KISSING HIS WIFE

Needing to prove the truth in the only means available, Gabriel determinedly leaned forward. Beatrice could deny the rightness of their being together with her words, but could she resist the power of the need that smoldered between them?

He had to discover if she could.

With a slow motion, he reached up to pluck the straw hat from her curls, nonchalantly tossing it aside.

Her lips parted in surprise. "Gabriel."

"Yes, Beatrice?" he murmured as he shifted to place one hand on each side of her hips and regarded those temptingly parted lips.

"What are you doing?"

"Making you a bit more comfortable."

"I am perfectly comfortable, thank you," she choked out.

"Good." He bent to lightly brush her mouth with his own. "So am I."

"Gabriel."

He gently nuzzled the corner of her mouth. "I am merely attempting to assure you that we have more in common than you are willing to admit."

She stiffened at his soft caress, but much to his satisfaction, she did not push him away.

"I do not think this is wise," she breathed.

"Do not think, my dear, merely feel," he urged, angling his head to claim her lips in a seeking kiss. . . .

Books by Debbie Raleigh

LORD CARLTON'S COURTSHIP

LORD MUMFORD'S MINX

A BRIDE FOR LORD CHALLMOND

A BRIDE FOR LORD WICKTON

A BRIDE FOR LORD BRASLEIGH

THE CHRISTMAS WISH

THE VALENTINE WISH

THE WEDDING WISH

A PROPER MARRIAGE

A CONVENIENT MARRIAGE

Published by Zebra Books

A CONVENIENT MARRIAGE

Debbie Raleigh

ZEBRA BOOKS
Kensington Publishing Corp.
http://www.kensingtonbooks.com

To John,
Who really does make fairy
tales come true

The Wedding

So this was love.

Whoever would have thought plain, awkward, eccentric Beatrice Chaswell would ever find such bliss? she thought as she heaved a giddy sigh.

No, no, she silently chastised herself. Not Beatrice Chaswell, but Countess of Faulconer, wife to the Earl of Faulconer.

Perhaps it was not so strange that she found it difficult to think of herself in such a title. She had barely been married two hours. And with her whirlwind courtship there had been little time before her marriage to actually consider anything beyond the immediate needs of acquiring a trousseau, calling the banns, and attending to the hundred and one details required for a wedding of such large proportions.

She still could not truly believe her incredible luck. Fairy tales happened to lovely, charming vixens who knew how to bewitch gentlemen with a smile. Not plodding, shy maidens who were far too plump for fashion and preferred pottering about her grandfather's workshop to dancing the waltz.

Gabriel was quite simply something out of her dreams.

Handsome, charming, witty, and heartbreakingly kind. He never made her feel clumsy or ugly. Never grimaced when she managed to wrinkle her gown or say something foolish in front of society. In truth, he was the only gentleman who had ever taken the effort to truly understand her.

He was her friend.

And soon he would be her lover.

That delicious thought made Beatrice impatiently glance around the elegant salon still crowded with her parents' guests. She would have far preferred a quiet ceremony with only a few close friends, but she had not had the heart to dampen her mother's enthusiasm. After three and a half seasons of watching her daughter suffer the embarrassment of being a perennial wallflower, Mrs. Chaswell had wanted to crow to the world that Beatrice had not only managed to land a husband, but a titled one at that. And for once her suitor's interest had not been firmly settled on the large inheritance that would one day be hers.

But now the ceremony was over and Beatrice had more than done her duty. All she wanted was to be alone with the gentleman who had made her believe in happily-ever-after.

The gentleman who had stolen her heart and changed her life forever.

Floating upon a cloud of euphoria, Beatrice began to weave her way through the babbling crowd, barely noting the envious glances and pointed stares at her waistline. She no longer had to concern herself with her parents' shallow friends and their barbed tongues. What did she care if they thought she had trapped Gabriel into marriage by becoming pregnant? Or even worse, that she had bought him with her dowry.

She was utterly indifferent to their spiteful dislike.

As long as she had Gabriel at her side, she could face anything.

Reaching the end of the salon with still no sight of her husband, Beatrice gave a faint frown.

Perhaps he was seeing to the carriage that would take them away from Surrey, she told herself. He was surely as eager as she to be away from the crowd.

Slipping through the door, she moved down the hall toward the front of the house. She had just passed the library, when she halted at the sound of deep voices drifting from behind a partially closed door.

At first she paused to see if she could recognize one of the voices as Gabriel's. Then it was the realization that the men were discussing her that kept her glued to her spot.

"To my mind, Beatrice got precisely what was coming to her."

"Damn right. Sticking her nose up in the air and pretending she would never stoop to marrying a poor bloke in need of a bit of the ready. Serves her right to have married the most desperate fortune hunter in London."

"Shame, though. All that lovely blunt being squandered on a destitute estate. Wish I'd seen through Faulconer's act before he swept the heiress off her feet. That money could have been mine."

"'Taint worth it, if you ask me. The woman is dicked in the nob, and not a thing to look at. Wouldn't want that in your bed every night."

"Don't think Faulconer will worry about bedding the chit. Now he has her fortune he can leave her buried at his godforsaken estate and have all the fun he wants in town. Damn his eyes. He is deuced lucky that my man of business didn't learn he was floundering in debt sooner. Gads, the man is said to owe every creditor in Derbyshire. Sweet little Beatrice wouldn't have been nearly so eager to tie the knot had she known the truth. Now it's too bloody late."

In the hall Beatrice walked to the front door and into the cold afternoon air.

She did not feel the bite of the wind, or the sting of the pelting sleet.

In truth she could feel nothing.

Her heart had just died.

Prologue

A long, eloquent silence filled the vicarage.

Standing to one side of the portrait he had just removed from its crate, Vicar Humbly watched his housekeeper frown at the faithful image of himself upon the canvas.

After nearly thirty years with Mrs. Stalwart beneath his roof, the vicar could easily read her expression of disapproval. Although the servant was fiercely loyal toward him, she could not always disguise her disappointment that he was not of a more stately nature.

He hid a smile as he returned his attention to the portrait, viewing his portly form and untidy gray hair with wry resignation. He had long ago accepted he would never possess the elegant pomp of a bishop or the dignified composure of a scholar. He appeared to be precisely what he was. A country vicar with no ambitions to be anything more.

Besides, this portrait had been no more than a ruse to help Addy in her marriage to Adam Drake. He had needed some legitimate excuse to linger in London long past the conventional visit, and he had been quite pleased with his clever notion to persuade Addy to paint his portrait.

A ruse that had worked to perfection, he silently preened.

There was no doubt that Addy and Adam's marriage had been in desperate straits. With Adam too stubborn to admit he had badly mishandled his spirited wife and Addy too resentful of being forced into marriage to realize her husband's many wonderful qualities, they had been living in a state of cold indifference. It had taken all of his ingenuity to at last break through their barriers and allow them to realize that they were indeed perfect for each other.

But he had succeeded, he acknowledged with a smug smile. The two were virtually inseparable with that rather giddy glow about them that spoke of abiding joy.

Now he could only hope he could work the same magic upon Beatrice and her new husband, Lord Faulconer.

After all, it had been the fact that he had received letters from Addy, Beatrice, and Victoria all on the same day that had prompted him to travel to London in the first place. He had been unable to shake the sense that the maidens were in need of his help. He had married all three of them despite his suspicion that none of them was entering marriage for the proper reasons. And he had known it was his duty to do what he could for his young friends before he could consider retiring to his lovely cottage.

His attempt to play Cupid had been remarkably effective with Addy. He could only pray he would have similar luck with Beatrice.

A loud sniff from Mrs. Stalwart put an end to his woolgathering, and with his singularly sweet smile he regarded his housekeeper with an expectant expression.

"Well, what do you think of it?"

The woman who ruled the rambling vicarage with an iron hand allowed her lips to thin.

"It certainly looks very much like you."

A condemning statement if he had ever heard one, Humbly acknowledged with a flare of amusement. He was careful, however, to keep his thoughts to himself. If truth be told, he was just the tiniest bit intimidated by the ruthlessly efficient woman.

"Yes," he murmured, "Addy is quite talented."

The woman waved a disapproving hand toward the canvas. "Do you not think it would be better if it were a bit more . . ."

"What?"

"A bit more noble?"

Humbly's lips twitched. "You mean if Addy had added more hair and fewer chins?"

She slashed him a chastising frown at his unseemly levity. "A vicar should have a measure of dignity."

Humbly sighed, knowing that Mrs. Stalwart would always be far more concerned for the status due his position than himself. He cared far more for people than church politics or neighborhood society.

"I am simply as God has made me, Mrs. Stalwart."

She lifted her brows as she took a knowing survey of his portly form.

"God and lemon tarts, Mr. Humbly," she corrected him in that tone that always made the vicar feel he was closer to six than sixty. "Do not think I am unaware of the large basket that arrived with the painting."

Humbly cast a guilty glance toward the desk where he had conveniently hidden the basket of lemon tarts Addy had been so kind to send. Dash it all, the housekeeper must have the nose of a hound to have sniffed out his secret stash.

"A mere trifling from Addy's kindly cook," he reluctantly confessed.

Mrs. Stalwart placed her hands upon her own ample

hips. "Had she been so kindly, she would have sent you cucumber sandwiches, not lemon tarts."

Humbly shuddered in horror.

He possessed a fervent loathing for cucumber sandwiches.

"You cannot propose that I be so ungrateful as to refuse such a generous gift?" he protested.

"The orphanage would no doubt appreciate the treats."

Although an extremely generous and kindly gentleman, Humbly did draw the line at handing over his beloved tarts.

A diversion was definitely in order.

"Ah, well, I believe we were discussing the portrait."

"Indeed," the housekeeper retorted in dry tones.

"It shall do very well," he continued, thinking of the portrait being hung in the long hall that held the portraits of all the previous vicars. "Perhaps it is not very noble, but it suits me."

"I suppose," Mrs. Stalwart reluctantly conceded.

Humbly's humor was readily restored by the woman's resigned expression.

"It could be worse." He could not help but tease. "Addy's mother, Lady Morrow, wished to have me painted with nothing more than a few angels and a fig leaf."

As predicted, the older woman's countenance flushed with annoyance.

"Lady Morrow? Dear heavens, the woman is without decency."

"You do not believe I should look rather noble in a fig leaf with an angel perched upon my shoulder?"

"Really, Vicar," the woman protested.

He gave a small chuckle at her predictable response. "Forgive me, Mrs. Stalwart. I was merely jesting, of course.

I asked Addy to paint my portrait precisely because I knew I could trust her to represent me in a truthful manner. I am not handsome, nor dignified nor particularly scholarly. I am a simple vicar with simple beliefs."

The stern expression swiftly softened at his words. "It is a fine portrait, Mr. Humbly," the housekeeper conceded. "And at least you are back in Surrey, where you belong. I cannot tell you how I fretted while you were in London. Such a dirty, dangerous place. I do not know how you could bear to stay for such a length of time."

Humbly smiled ruefully. In truth, he had cared very little for London. And even less for the elegant society events he had attended. He had discovered them to be overcrowded, stifling affairs that had usually offered nothing more than a pounding headache and crushed toes by the end of the evening.

Of course, there had been that charming monkey who had terrified the maidens into shrieking flight, he recalled with a less than saintly flare of amusement.

"Ah, well, it was quite an experience. And to be honest, there were more than a few moments when I wished for nothing more than to be in my comfortable library with a pot of your special tea."

Mrs. Stalwart tried to disguise her flare of pleasure at his words behind a stern glance.

"So I should think. It is unnatural to be gadding about the country in such a fashion."

"Yes."

"And now that you have returned you must think upon arranging your belongings. The new vicar will be arriving in just a few months. I cannot be expected to pack all those musty books you insist on taking to your cottage."

"Certainly not," Humbly was swift to agree, then he offered the formidable woman an apologetic smile. "However, I fear the books will have to wait."

Mrs. Stalwart turned her considerable bulk to face him squarely. "You are not returning to London," she said in flat tones.

"No, no." The vicar tugged at his crumpled cravat. "Actually I am off to Derbyshire."

"Derbyshire?" She managed to place enough disdain in her voice to imply he was headed directly for the netherworld. "Whatever would possess you to go to Derbyshire?"

"Dear, sweet Beatrice," he readily confided.

"Miss Chaswell?"

Humbly gave a faint sigh, knowing it would be difficult to think of Beatrice as anything but Miss Chaswell. She had grown up less than a mile from the vicarage and Humbly had known her from the day she had been brought into this world.

His eyes slightly dimmed at the memory of the awkward, diffident child she had been. Despite her social position and large fortune, life had not been easy for Beatrice. Not only had she been painfully shy, but there was no denying her short, plump form and regular features could make no claim to beauty. She was consistently overlooked at balls and assemblies by the local beaus, and rarely recalled when the young members of society gathered for their casual parties.

It had only made matters worse that her parents were undoubtedly blessed with both beauty and social acclaim. It was as if a wren had been slipped into a nest of brilliant peacocks, leaving all baffled as to how the mix-up could have occurred.

Not that she hadn't been loved, Humbly was swift to remind himself. Both Mr. and Mrs. Chaswell had doted upon their only child. But there was no mistaking they could never quite understand Beatrice, nor fully appreciate her extraordinary intelligence that had been a gift from her grandfather.

They desired a daughter they could dangle before society like a pretty bauble, and instead received a plain, studious child who preferred inventions to society.

He heaved a faint sigh.

He had hoped that someday Beatrice would discover a gentleman who would teach her to appreciate her many fine qualities. A man who would love her so deeply that she could appreciate how rare and wonderful she truly was.

Instead, he very much feared that the Earl of Faulconer had courted the poor child for the same reason she had ever been courted by gentlemen.

Her indecently large dowry.

He sighed again, his heart heavy with concern.

"She is now Lady Faulconer, Mrs. Stalwart," he corrected the housekeeper in sad tones.

She frowned with impatience. "Surely if Lady Faulconer is in need of a vicar she can discover one closer to Derbyshire?"

"I believe she is more in need of a friend than a vicar. And I do count myself as her friend."

Perhaps sensing his unease, Mrs. Stalwart deepened her frown.

"Has something occurred? Is she not well?"

"That is what I intend to discover."

Watching his soft features harden with uncharacteristic determination, the servant heaved a resigned sigh.

"Well, I do not care for you gallivanting about all of England in this manner. It cannot be healthy for a gentleman of your years."

Feeling rather like Methuselah, Humbly smiled with wry amusement.

"Do not fear. Soon I shall be comfortably established in my lovely cottage with nothing more pressing upon my delicate constitution than a walk through the garden."

"I do not like this," his housekeeper muttered in dark tones. "'Tis unnatural, I tell you."

Humbly did not disagree with the woman's sentiments.

He was at heart a gentleman who deeply appreciated the familiarity of his shabby vicarage and comfort of his own bed. The very last thing he desired was jolting his old bones so far across the country.

But he was also a gentleman who knew his duty.

He had wed Beatrice to Lord Faulconer.

He had to ensure that they were happy together.

The vicar sighed again.

He was beginning to develop a sincere sympathy for the plight of poor Cupid.

One

"My heavens, such a racket. Not that I am complaining, dear Gabriel. Goodness knows a woman in my position would never consider bemoaning her lot in life. It is our Christian duty to be pleased with whatever may befall us. And in truth, Beatrice is such a dear child, I cannot begrudge her peculiar little hobby. I would wish, however, that she would not allow those nasty tradesmen to traipse through the grounds until a decent hour."

With a deep sense of reluctance, Gabriel Baxtor, Earl of Faulconer, set aside his morning paper to regard his aunt Sarah as she fluttered into the room. A delicate woman with gray hair, she was appropriately attired in black as befitting her role as a much put upon martyr.

As a rule Gabriel endured her sweet complaints with the same wry resignation as he endured the flood of workmen repairing the tumbledown estate and open distrust of his numerous tenants.

After the sudden death of his father and older brother when their yacht had so unexpectedly sunk in the Channel, he had not fully realized the burdens he would be shouldering.

The previous Earl of Faulconer was a renowned reprobate with far more interest in pursuing pleasure than tending to his faltering estate. His eldest son had followed in his footsteps with a commendable vengeance, gambling away what little money remained and borrowing heavily against the future income of Falcon Park.

Gabriel had washed his hands of both of them when he was barely seventeen. He had discovered no pleasure in the scandalous parties his father had hosted, nor the dubious characters who had clung to the fringes of his father's society. In truth, he was heartily shamed by his family's hedonistic lifestyle and unable to bear the sight of the noble house tumbling into disrepair while the tenants suffered more desperately each passing year.

Perhaps cowardly he had chosen to enter the army rather than watch the painful decline of the proud Faulconer name. He wanted no part of the inevitable plunge into poverty that would destroy literally hundreds of lives.

It had never occurred to him that his feckless father and brother would be taken from this world together. And that he would be left to face the disaster as Earl of Faulconer.

The truth had not struck until he had returned to an empty Falcon Park with no one to greet him beyond a desperate Aunt Sarah and a hundred resentful tenants who looked to him to restore the glory of Falcon Park.

Gabriel gave a small shake of his head, his lean features tanned from the hours he worked in the fields hardening to grim lines.

He had been shocked and terrified to discover the sheer depth of his father's folly. Not only had he bled the estate dry, he had sold every piece of jewelry and work of art that might have bought Gabriel time to consider the mess he was in. He was well and truly on the dun without hope of seeing a return on the estate unless a large influx of cash appeared with which to plant the fields and replace the tools that had fallen into disrepair in the nearly collapsed barn.

Beyond that had been the ghastly state of the manor house and numerous cottages not fit for the rats, let alone his tenants.

He had to act.

And he had to act swiftly.

Which is precisely what he had done.

His grim features became even more grim as the late May sunlight glinted off the rich copper highlights in his auburn hair.

Like any fine gentleman in dire straits, he had hurried himself off to London and wooed the most likely heiress he could discover. It was the only respectable means of restoring his estate. Especially for a gentleman with no skills beyond the battlefield. And in short order he had achieved his goal.

He had wed the wealthy Miss Beatrice Chaswell and in just a few short months his entire estate had seen the benefits of her vast fortune.

The cottages were newly repaired, the fields were being planted, and even the manor house was being completely restored.

It had all worked out precisely as he had desperately hoped it would.

And he had never been so miserable in his entire life.

Realizing that his aunt was regarding him with an expectant expression, Gabriel thrust aside his dark broodings and forced the muscles of his countenance to relax.

He had made his choice and now he must accept the cost.

"Good morning, Aunt Sarah," he managed in neutral tones.

"I suppose all that knocking and banging woke you up as well, poor boy," the older woman chattered as she moved to the sideboard and began filling her plate.

"Actually I have been up for several hours. I am told the hay is sweeter when cut in May, so we have been doing our best to complete the task."

"Indeed? How nice. I see there are no eggs again this morning. Ah, well, I shall simply make do with toast." Aunt Sarah heaved a mournful sigh, then managed to load her plate with ham, kippers, and a vast assortment of other delicacies before taking her place at the table. She gave a delicate wince at the distant sound of metal scraping against metal. "Really, Gabriel, all that noise. It cannot be good for your digestion. Perhaps I should speak with Beatrice? Just to put a small flea in her ear that you would be better satisfied—"

"No," Gabriel interrupted sharply.

The older woman was clearly taken aback. "Pardon me?"

"It pleases Beatrice to seek out the latest inventions. I will not have her disturbed."

With a self-depreciating flutter of her hands, Aunt Sarah gave a weak smile.

"Oh, no, certainly not. And I must say, Gabriel, you are a wonderfully indulgent husband. Not many a gentleman would so generously allow his wife to pursue such an odd fancy."

Gabriel felt the familiar twist of pain as he thought of his wife. Before their marriage she had regarded him with such a glow of happiness. She had been so sweet, so trusting. And he had been so determined to ensure that she never be disappointed in him.

But, of course, fate was never so kind.

They had barely exchanged their vows, when she had managed to overhear the whispers of his desperate straits. She had suddenly understood his insistence for their swift marriage and determination to sweep her to Derbyshire with all possible haste.

And with that understanding had come a deep, unwavering hatred toward her new husband.

A hatred that had in no way lessened over the past weeks.

"Oh, yes, I am quite indulgent," he said in dry tones.

Aunt Sarah gave a delicate sniff. "I do not believe Beatrice fully appreciates her good fortune in having you as her husband."

Gabriel gave a humorless laugh. "I assure you, Aunt Sarah, that Beatrice fully realizes her fortune in becoming Lady Faulconer. Which is precisely why I wish to indulge her. A wife should receive something from her husband."

"How very droll you are this morning, my dear," the older woman retorted, as always blithely indifferent to the knowledge that it was because of Beatrice she had food to eat and a dry bed to sleep in. "As if Beatrice isn't honored by becoming a countess. It is, in truth, more than she deserves with her grandfather being in trade. Not all gentlemen would overlook such an unfortunate connection."

Gabriel abruptly rose to his feet, his nose flaring with distaste at his aunt's snobbish tones. Lucifer's teeth. They had been living hand to mouth until the arrival of Beatrice and her grandfather's money. It was outrageous to pretend they had done the young maiden some great favor in dragging her to a shabby home with a leaking roof and no servants.

"You are wrong, Aunt," he said between clenched teeth. "There were literally hundreds of gentlemen desiring a connection with Beatrice."

Oblivious to the edge of warning in his tone, Aunt Sarah smiled in a complacent fashion.

"And you cut them all out, did you not? Such a clever boy."

"Oh, yes, I am all that is clever." He gave a half bow. "Excuse me. I must meet with my steward."

Thoroughly annoyed with his obtuse aunt and himself for allowing his rigidly controlled emotions to be ruffled, Gabriel strided out of the room and down the long hall.

For once he did not shudder at the tattered carpeting or faded tapestries. Instead, he attempted to focus his thoughts on the vast amount of work awaiting his attention.

When he had been in the army he had never considered the difficulties of being a farmer. To his mind you dropped a few seeds in the ground and allowed nature to take its course.

Now he could only laugh at his naivety. Not only was farming grueling labor and constant worry, but he had discovered the estate was woefully behind on the latest techniques. Over the past months he had diligently sought to teach himself the best methods of improving production and protecting his land from being drained of its nutrients, but he knew he was still lacking in experience.

It was frustrating to consider the years he had wasted upon the battlefield. Had he known what would be expected of him, he would have devoted himself to learning all that was possible of land management. As it was, he was constantly struggling not to appear a complete buffoon.

With a click of his tongue at his futile wishing, Gabriel headed down the stairs, only to come to a startled halt at the sight of his wife.

Although it was still early, her sensible gray gown was already streaked with dirt and the trim at her hem dangled upon the polished oak stairs. Even the soft honey hair had managed to escape the knot atop her head and curled about the sweetly rounded face.

Gabriel swallowed a smile of amusement at Beatrice's disheveled appearance. She could never claim the traditional beauty with her numerous curves and plain features, but he found a decided charm to her air of blithe indifference to fashion.

This was a rare woman without vanity or a slavish devotion to fashion. Her thoughts were consumed by far more important matters.

His brief amusement, however, was swiftly squashed as the dark amber eyes hardened at the sight of his lean form.

"Beatrice," he murmured, knowing she was quite likely to sweep past him without ever acknowledging his presence. Since arriving at Falcon Park she had managed to avoid him with splendid ease. Only the undoubted changes throughout the house assured him that she had not bolted long ago.

Coming to a reluctant halt, she regarded him with a stiff expression.

"Good morning, my lord."

There was no mistaking the sudden chill in the air, but Gabriel gamely sought to reach out to his stubborn wife.

"Have you eaten breakfast?"

"Not as yet."

"I would suggest you avoid the breakfast room," he generously warned. "Aunt Sarah is in rare form."

She gave a faint shrug. "I am just to my room to change. I promised the vicar I would call upon Mrs. Patton."

A frown gathered on Gabriel's brow. Although he rarely saw his wife, he was well aware she was a frequent visitor among the tenants. So frequent that he feared she was pressing herself far too hard to make life better for others.

"You mustn't allow him to run you ragged, my dear," he said in careful tones. "I am certain one of the footmen could easily take a basket of food to the widow."

"It is my duty, my lord," she retorted in icy tones.

Gabriel felt himself stiffen at her deliberate barb.

Duty.

Oh, yes.

He had endured a stomach full of duty.

It was what had gotten him into this mess in the first place.

"Of course. We all have our duty, do we not?"

She flushed at his mocking tones. "As you say."

"I will not keep you."

"Good day, my lord."

Instantly regretting the knowledge he had once again wasted the opportunity to break through the ice between them, Gabriel laid a hand upon her arm.

"Beatrice."

She firmly backed from his touch, but she halted to regard him with a lift of her honey brows.

"Yes?"

"Will you join us for dinner this evening?"

"Are there to be guests?"

"Not that I am aware of. However, it would be a nice change to have my wife at the table."

"I prefer a tray in my room, my lord."

Gabriel battled his flare of impatience. He remembered a time when she had rushed to be in his presence. When those amber eyes had sparked to sudden life when he simply walked into the room.

She could not have completely buried those feelings for him, could she? Somewhere deep inside her she still had to care.

Why must she make this so bloody unbearable for both of them?

"How long do you intend to play this game, Beatrice?" he demanded. "Surely I have been punished long enough?"

Her gaze abruptly narrowed. "It is no game, sir."

"Of course it is. You hide from me like a petulant child."

"You were the one who desired this marriage. Please do not complain now that it is not precisely as you envisioned it to be."

His lips twisted as he recalled his foolish dreams. In his imaginings Beatrice was a loving wife who never discovered his need for her fortune, while he gallantly devoted himself to her happiness.

Foolish dreams that had been ended before they could even begin.

"I recall that you were more than eager for marriage as well, my dear."

Something that might have been pain fluttered over her pale features until she rigidly schooled her expression to stern lines.

"Yes, but unlike you, I have learned to accept what a ghastly mistake it was."

He gave a slow shake of his head. "It need not be a mistake. We could make this marriage as comfortable as any other. More comfortable than most with a little effort."

"A marriage based on lies can never be more than a hollow mockery."

He heaved a frustrated sigh. "I never lied to you, Beatrice. You may not lay that upon my door."

She remained unimpressed by his strict diligence in avoiding any direct lie during their swift courtship.

"Did you not, my lord? At the very least you misrepresented yourself."

He narrowed his hazel eyes. "And how did I misrepresent myself?"

"You pretended to care."

Gabriel flinched at the dark accusation. "And how can you be so certain that I did not?"

She abruptly averted her face to regard the dark paneling that lined the staircase.

"Had you cared, you would have told me the truth from the beginning."

His hands clenched at his sides. He had gone over the courtship in his mind a hundred times. On each occasion he had questioned what he could have done differently. And on each occasion the answer had been the same.

He had done the only thing possible.

"And you would never have allowed me to even approach you again," he said in flat tones.

"At least we would have been spared this disaster."

He longed to reach out and shake some sense into her. How could she desire to live in this uncomfortable fashion?

"It is too late for regrets." He reached out to gently turn her to face him. As always, he was startled by the soft satin of her warm skin. So smooth and utterly tempting. "We are wed and should make the best of the situation."

She was swift to jerk from his touch. "Easy for you to say, my lord. You have what you desire."

He gave a humorless laugh. "Do you think so?"

"You have your fortune."

"And what is it you desire, Beatrice?"

"To be left in peace. Excuse me."

With determined movements she turned to continue her ascent up the stairs. Gabriel allowed her to retreat, knowing from bitter experience that it was impossible to force her to listen to his words of sense.

He had done everything possible to make Beatrice comfortable at Falcon Park.

He had allowed her to choose her suite of rooms far from his own.

He had encouraged her to begin meeting with various inventors around the countryside who hoped to gain her patronage.

And most important of all, he had never pressed her to provide him with his husbandly rights to her bed.

Not that she had shown the least gratitude for his efforts, he acknowledged darkly.

She had labeled him the enemy and he was beginning to fear that nothing would change her mind.

Much to her disgust, Beatrice realized that she was trembling as she entered her chamber and closed the door.

Saints above.

It had been months since she had discovered Gabriel's treachery.

Why could she not meet with her husband without feeling as if her heart were being ripped from her bosom?

Because you possessed the poor taste to tumble into love with the man, a voice mocked in the back of her mind.

She winced as she paced across the refurbished room she had decorated in a pale yellow and ivory.

What a fool she had been.

For years she had realized that she was destined to be the target of fortune hunters. No maiden could be heir to such an embarrassing legacy without attracting the attention of unwelcome scoundrels. Especially a maiden who so clearly lacked the grace and beauty to capture the heart of a gentleman in the position to wed for love.

But perhaps arrogantly, she had believed herself far too intelligent to be swept off her feet by a common rogue.

She was no simpering debutant to be charmed by sweet words and practiced kisses.

Oh, no, Beatrice Chaswell was far too clever for any fortune hunter.

She abruptly closed her eyes as a shudder racked her body. Gabriel had taught her that she was not nearly as clever as she believed.

It was easy to be alert for insincere flattery and the usual ploys to lure her into a compromising situation. How could she possibly have prepared herself for a gentleman who claimed to be her friend?

Beatrice reached the window overlooking the neglected garden, when a soft knock on the door had her absently smoothing the stained skirts as she moved back across the room. She rarely took notice of her appearance, since no amount of lovely gowns nor elegant coiffeurs were going to improve her lack of beauty. Besides, she could hardly study the variety of machines brought for her inspection without becoming a bit grubby.

Opening the door, she discovered the downstairs maid waiting for her in the hall.

"Pardon me, my lady." The servant dipped a small curtsy.

"What is it, Hilda?"

"There is a gentleman to see you."

Beatrice gave a small frown. The household staff had been well trained to ensure that the numerous inventors eager to gain her patronage were seen only during the early morning hours.

"Did you tell him that I only see tradesmen by appointment? Have him speak with Mr. Eaton," she commanded, mentioning her highly efficient secretary.

"He is not a tradesman, ma'am. It is a Vicar Humbly," Hilda corrected her mistress.

Beatrice widened her eyes in surprise. "Vicar Humbly?"

"I believe that was the name he gave."

A warm rush of pleasure raced through Beatrice. Dear, sweet Mr. Humbly. Until that moment she did not realize precisely how much she had missed his amusing bumblings and odd flashes of insight that came without warning. Although older than her own father, he was one of the few people she felt thoroughly comfortable to be around.

Perhaps because she never felt as if he were judging her and finding her wanting. Or because he truly appeared to appreciate her talents, which were far from maidenly.

Whatever the reason, Beatrice could not deny a deep sense of pleasure at the thought of seeing him again.

"Where did you ask him to wait?"

"In the front parlor."

"Tell him I shall be right down," Beatrice commanded. "And call for tea."

"Yes, ma'am."

Beatrice was struck by a sudden thought. "Oh, and, Hilda, make sure that Cook has plenty of cakes upon the tray. Vicar Humbly possesses a love for sweets."

"Very good."

With an excitement she had not felt since arriving at Falcon Park, Beatrice rushed to change her gown to one of pale rose and struggled to tame her willful honey curls into a semblance of tidiness. She even recalled to wash the lingering dirt from her hands and flushed countenance.

There was nothing to be done to make her appear taller or more elegant. Certainly nothing could be done to make her appear to be a countess.

She looked like a farmer's daughter, and no dresses or pretty ribbons would ever alter that depressing fact.

With a grimace at the reflection in the mirror, Beatrice firmly turned and headed for the door.

She had determined long ago not to regret what she would never be. She was nothing if not practical.

Entering the hall, Beatrice briskly moved toward the stairs. When she had first arrived at Falcon Park she had been horrified to discover the disreputable condition of the ancient estate. Built with a heavily ornate Gothic influence, it possessed a large gatehouse, charming lodges, and a cast iron conservatory. Inside, however, it was dark and damp with furnishings that had long ago fallen beyond repair.

For the first week she had simply wandered the vast halls with a sick sense of regret. Not only at the realization that her marriage to Gabriel was a mockery, but that the home she had always dreamed of possessing had turned out to be a pile of molding rocks.

Hardly the stuff of fairy tales.

Then common sense had taken over. She might not be able to return Gabriel to her knight in shining armor, but she could restore Falcon Park to its former glory.

With her usual efficiency she had set about hiring a workforce from the local area and sent to London for a variety of architects and artists to advise the workers upon the delicate task of repairing the ravages of time and neglect without destroying the precious history of the building.

First had been the private chambers, of course. Beatrice found no charm in having the rain dripping upon her head while she lay in her bed. And then the kitchen and servants' quarters, which she had swiftly filled with the necessary staff to keep the large house in comfort.

The chapel and dining room were currently under siege as well as the gardens, which she had ordered to be terraced with a wide path to the distant lake.

Oddly, Gabriel had not protested her complete invasion of his home. Even when Aunt Sarah had slyly attempted to stir his anger with her sweet insults of Beatrice's managing habits, he had merely cast the older woman a steely gaze and informed her that the Countess of Faulconer was in full and complete charge of the household, as it should be.

For a dangerous moment Beatrice had felt her anger momentarily waver. In that brief, shining breath he had once again been the engaging companion who had won her heart. The man who gazed at her not with pity or greed but with a deep understanding of who she was inside.

Beatrice found her steps faltering before she was sternly continuing her path to the front parlor. Saints above, had she not already learned the truth of the Earl of Faulconer?

He had wed her for her fortune.

His ability to make her feel as if she could be so much more to his life than a mere means to saving his estate was not a ruse she would fall for again.

Clearing her futile thoughts, Beatrice pushed open the door to the parlor and stepped inside. The room was dark and highly vaulted with a profusion of pilasters and arched windows. Unfortunately the once-ornate furnishings had become threadbare and dull with age.

But seated like a bright ray of light upon a high-backed chair was Vicar Humbly with his mussed hair, his wrinkled coat, and a smile that could lift the heaviest of hearts.

"Mr. Humbly," she breathed, rushing forward to throw herself in his arms as he awkwardly rose to his feet.

Sweet comfort flooded through her as he gently patted her back and then stepped away to regard her with his soft brown gaze.

"Beatrice, my dear, how delightful it is to see you again."

"Whatever are you doing in Derbyshire?"

An expression of near comic dismay descended upon his round countenance.

"Oh, dear, not again."

Beatrice blinked in surprise. "Pardon me?"

"I was so certain that I had sent a letter warning you of my impending visit." He heaved a resigned sigh. "No doubt it is still sitting upon my desk, awaiting me to post it. I fear, my dearest, that I become only more absentminded as I grow older. A frightening prospect, is it not?"

Beatrice chuckled at his droll tone. Rather to her amazement, she realized just how good it felt to do so. It had been far too long since she had been amused by anything.

"Never mind. It is a most delightful surprise."

"How very kind of you."

"Nonsense," she insisted, taking his arm and firmly leading him to a nearby sofa. Pressing him onto the tattered cushions, she settled beside him. "It is a joy to have a houseguest. You are my first, you know."

"Am I?" Humbly gave a wry smile. "Well, I suppose it is hardly proper to intrude upon a newlywed couple. I only beg you will not think me entirely without sensibilities."

Beatrice stiffened despite her best intentions. To think

of herself as a dewy-eyed bride desperate to be alone with her husband was ludicrous.

"I assure you that you do not intrude," she said firmly. "Indeed, you will be a most welcome distraction. Lord Faulconer is quite busy restoring the fields and cottages."

Thankfully accepting her blithe response for the lack of desire to be private with her husband, Humbly glanced about the vast chamber.

"I understand his desire to restore Falcon Park. It is a lovely estate. A fine parkland and such a beautiful home."

Beatrice gave a faint grimace. "I fear it is all sadly in disrepair."

"Nothing that cannot be put right," he assured her with a sweet smile. "'Commit your work to the Lord, and your plans will be established.'"

Beatrice discovered herself easily laughing once again. "Actually we have committed the work to a small army of workmen whom you will swiftly discover manage to be underfoot at the most inconvenient times."

The sherry-brown eyes twinkled with amusement. "Ah, but think of the result."

It was something Beatrice pondered quite often. No matter what her reason for being at Falcon Park, she knew that she would take great pride once the work was complete. Having such a personal hand in the repairs had formed a bond with the house she would never have expected.

"Yes, I have hopes it shall all be worthwhile in the end."

He regarded her with an oddly knowing expression. "All things that are worthwhile require the most sacrifice."

"Yes," she murmured, although she sensed he referred to more than replacing rotting roofs and delicate stained glass windows. It was rather a relief when the door opened and the maid entered to place a large tray on the table before the sofa. "Thank you, Hilda," she murmured as the servant bobbed a curtsy and left the room. Pouring them both a cup of the suitably hot tea, she loaded a plate of various pastries for the vicar. "You will note I have not forgotten your fondness for sweets, Mr. Humbly."

The vicar beamed with pleasure as he readily accepted his plate. "How very kind. Oh, my, are those lemon tarts?"

"I believe they are."

"Heavenly," he murmured as he took a large bite of the tart.

Settling back on the lumpy cushions, Beatrice regarded her guest with an open curiosity.

"Now, why do you not tell me what brings you to Derbyshire?"

"Well, I wished to see you, of course, my dear. And I have an old friend not far from here whom I wished to visit. Unfortunately he is not well and I could not in good conscience impose myself upon his household."

She smiled in sympathy. "I am sorry your friend is unwell, but very pleased you will be staying at Falcon Park."

Humbly efficiently polished off his last tart and reached for another. "I do hope your husband will be similarly pleased. I am, after all, a mere stranger to him."

In truth Beatrice had not even considered her husband's reaction.

"Do not fear, Lord Faulconer will be delighted to have you as our guest," she said with more confidence than she felt. "More tea?"

"No, thank you. But perhaps one more of those tarts?"

"Of course." Beatrice refilled his plate and watched in pleasure as he rapidly consumed the last tart. Thank goodness she had managed to lure a seasoned cook from the local squire. "Tell me how Mrs. Stalwart goes on."

Humbly wrinkled his nose. "Very well, although quite vexed with me at the moment."

Beatrice did not doubt that the overly protective woman was decidedly miffed to have her chick so far from her nest.

"She did not desire you to travel such a great distance from Surrey?"

"Precisely." Humbly gave a sigh. "One would think that I had suggested sailing to the colonies."

"Well, it is a goodly distance."

The twinkle returned to his eyes. "Especially for a man of my advanced years."

"Nonsense." She was swift to protest. This man would never grow old. Not with his youthful spirit.

"Well, that was not her only complaint. You see, my dear, I am under very strict orders to have my library sorted through so that my books can be packed and moved to my cottage."

"Your cottage? You are leaving the vicarage?" she demanded in startled tones.

"Oh, yes, I am soon to retire."

Beatrice felt a poignant pang of loss. There had always been something very comforting in having Mr. Humbly at the vicarage. A constant in an ever-changing world.

"But that is dreadful."

"Oh, no, my dear, it is entirely for the best," he said in mild tones. "I grow old and tired and quite looking forward to my days shuffling through my garden and relaxing by the fire with no fear I shall be called out by one of my flock. Besides, the new vicar is quite an exceptional gentleman. I do not doubt that the Church will be in competent hands."

"But it will not be you," she said sadly.

Before he could retort, the door was once again pushed open. Expecting Hilda returning to collect the tea tray, Beatrice froze in surprise as the elegant form of her husband stepped into the room.

A tingle of awareness she could not entirely banish despite her fierce attempts rushed through her body. Although he was casually attired in buff breeches and tan coat, he still managed to have an air of coiled power about him. It was in the graceful precision of his movements and authority etched onto the features just a breath from being beautiful.

There was no wonder she had tumbled for him like a giddy schoolgirl, she thought ruefully. Few gentlemen could measure up to Gabriel in looks or charm.

Especially when he had combined his natural attributes with stolen kisses that had made her blood rush and her knees weak.

Thankfully unaware of her inward musings, Gabriel strolled forward and regarded Vicar Humbly with a curious glance.

"I was told that we have a visitor. May I welcome you to Falcon Park?"

Two

"Thank you, my lord."

Gabriel found the tension that had clutched at his body when he had discovered an old acquaintance had called upon his wife slowly easing. He was not certain what he had expected. Perhaps one of her old suitors hoping to ease her obvious disappointment in her husband. Or an interfering friend who would attempt to convince her to return to the comfort of her home in Surrey.

He now felt rather foolish to discover it was only Beatrice's old vicar, who had performed their wedding ceremony.

Certainly his arrival had not been worthy of Gabriel's swift retreat from the fields and his hasty charge through the house, he wryly acknowledged. He had not moved with such determination since leaving Napoleon's battlefields.

"How delightful," he murmured, performing an elegant bow.

The older gentleman struggled to push his bulk from the sofa.

"You must forgive me, my lord," he puffed, absently attempting to tame the handful of determined gray hairs. "It appears that the letter warning of my impending arrival was never delivered. No doubt because it is still sitting on my desk. I fear I have simply descended with my hat in hand."

Gabriel's lips twitched at his dry tone. "Think nothing of it, Mr. Humbly. We are pleased to have you here."

"So kind."

"Not at all." Gabriel turned his gaze to his wife, startled to discover her lovely eyes glowing with a warmth he had not seen for far too long. He felt a momentary pang of jealousy that it was not he who had created that glow before sternly gathering control of his futile emotions. "I do hope that Beatrice has warned you that we have been invaded by a small army of workmen?"

The vicar gave a nod of his head. "Yes, indeed. May I say, this is a truly lovely home? No doubt there is a great deal of history within these stone walls?"

Gabriel's lips twisted as he recalled the dubious history of the Faulconer clan. For one of England's finest families, there was an embarrassing profusion of scoundrels, gamesters, and even a few outright criminals.

"Most of it is best not remembered," he admitted. "I fear my ancestors were a motley crew."

Far from shocked by his lack of snobbish pretensions, the vicar merely chuckled.

"I am certain that most of us could find a few undesirables among our distant relatives. I have it upon excellent authority that my great-uncle was hanged at Tyburn as a highwayman."

Gabriel discovered himself oddly drawn to this peculiar gentleman. There was a simple charm about him as well as a faint hint of shrewd intelligence deep in his eyes.

"If you are truly interested, I believe there are a few books in the library that trace the history of Falcon Park."

The vicar appeared suitably pleased. "Thank you. I

should enjoy that very much. History has always been rather an interest of mine."

"Mine as well." Gabriel slid a glance toward his silent wife. "Beatrice, on the other hand, has her mind firmly on the future."

As happened all too frequently, Beatrice stiffened at his attempt to forge a bridge between them, but Mr. Humbly was swift to fill the awkward silence.

"Ah, yes, I remember how fascinated Beatrice has always been in the latest inventions."

"It is how my grandfather amassed his fortune," she said in low tones.

Gabriel flinched at the direct hit, but Humbly merely smiled.

"A very astute gentleman with a rare gift of realizing the potential of various inventions long before others could see their worth. It always amazed me how he could look at what appeared to me as nothing more than gears and wheels and see magic."

"It is a gift he has bestowed upon his granddaughter," Gabriel said, carefully noting the startled glance he received from his wife. "She regularly allows hopeful inventors to display their work in the hope of her patronage."

His instinct was correct when the vicar clapped his hands together rather than express the disapproval poor Beatrice had endured too often.

"But that is wonderful."

Delightfully flustered, Beatrice could not prevent the color from flooding her cheeks. It added a decided charm to her plain features.

"I do not claim to possess my grandfather's talent, but I do enjoy the thought of encouraging those who will keep England at the forefront of the world."

"A most admirable sentiment. I hope you will include

me in your fascinating hobby," the vicar retorted with obvious sincerity.

Beatrice gave a wry grimace. "If you wish, although I must warn you that more often than not it is all nothing more than a mare's nest. When there is money offered, every scoundrel and ruffian is eager to line up at the door."

Humbly gave a wise nod of his head. "Yes, I suppose that is true enough."

"It only makes it worse that I happen to be a woman," Beatrice continued, her light tone not quite disguising her inner frustration at the prejudice she consistently faced. "Too many gentlemen possess the belief that because I wear a dress I cannot possibly also possess a brain."

"A notion you are swift to correct, I am certain, my dear," Gabriel said in dry tones.

Her gaze abruptly dropped. "I should hope so. I would not wish to be thought a fool."

Again.

The word went unsaid, but it hung in the air with a thick vengeance. Gabriel tightened his lips.

Did the most simple conversations need be plagued with animosity? Could she not lower that prickly guard even a moment?

It appeared not, he conceded with an unconsciously weary shake of his head.

Well, he had plenty of troubles awaiting his attention that he could attempt to solve. There was little use in battering his head against a stone wall.

"No, such a dreadful fate when one is foolish," he drawled before turning back to encounter the vicar's speculative gaze. "Mr. Humbly, I hope you will make yourself comfortable. Beatrice, I shall see you later."

About to make a dignified exit, Gabriel was halted as the portly gentleman stepped toward him.

"My lord?"

"Yes?"

"If you do not mind, I would desire to ensure that the young farmer who so kindly brought me from the posting inn has been fed. He refused my offer of payment for his troubles and I would like to think he has received something for his efforts."

"Of course. We shall go directly to the kitchen."

Gabriel patiently waited for Humbly to take leave of Beatrice before escorting him out of the room. He did not doubt it appeared odd that he made no effort to bid his own wife farewell, but at the moment he did not trust his temper to endure yet another barb from her sharp tongue.

Walking down the long hall, Gabriel drew in a deep breath and glanced toward the much-shorter gentleman, who was currently craning his neck to regard the long corridor.

"Oh my, an open-timbered hallway," Humbly breathed with sincere delight. "So lovely."

Never having been in the position of host, Gabriel gathered his thoughts and made an effort to appear suitably pleased with his guest.

"It is, I believe, one of the finer halls in all of Derbyshire," he said as they moved toward the stairs. "Of course, like the rest of the estate, it has been shamefully neglected."

"I suppose not all people appreciate the difficulties of preserving history," the vicar said in mild tones.

"No, indeed." Gabriel briefly thought of his father's bitter complaints at the drafty rooms and rambling wings. "Had my father had his way, he would have pulled this monstrosity down and built an Italian villa. Thankfully the entail precluded such drastic changes."

The vicar sucked in a sharp breath, not entirely able to disguise his shocked disapproval at the late earl's lack of appreciation for his inheritance. Gabriel knew he would be even more shocked by the nights of gambling and dissipation that had left the rooms in shambles and priceless furnishings toppled about like worthless bits of rubbish.

"Good heavens. It would be a sin to destroy such beauty," Humbly said with a shake of his head.

"My thought precisely," Gabriel readily agreed, although deep inside he shuddered at the cost of saving such beauty.

He and Beatrice both had been sacrificed upon the altar of Falcon Park.

Almost as if able to read his thoughts, Vicar Humbly abruptly turned his head to regard him with a searching gaze.

"No doubt Beatrice was delighted when she arrived? Not all brides can claim such an ancient countryseat."

Gabriel grimaced as they made their way down the stairs and he turned to lead his guest toward the back of the house.

"I am not sure *delighted* is precisely how I would describe her reaction."

"Overwhelmed, perhaps?"

Gabriel paused before giving a faint shrug. If this gentleman were to remain at Falcon Park, he would swiftly discover that all was not well between Lord and Lady Faulconer.

"Closer to furious, I fear."

Humbly gave a vague blink. "Furious?"

Gabriel shrugged. "Beatrice had not realized the full extent of my father's reckless disregard for his inheritance. No bride would be delighted to discover leaking roofs, fireplaces that smoke, and only an old retainer to see to her needs."

"Ah." There was a wealth of understanding in that one word. "You did not warn her of what to expect?"

Gabriel's hands unconsciously clenched at his sides. "No. A decision I assure you that I deeply regret."

"Honesty is always best between man and wife, no matter how difficult," the vicar murmured.

"Rather easier said than done."

"Indeed." There was a measure of silence before Humbly sent him a startlingly kind smile. "But do not worry. I am certain that Beatrice has quite settled in and will soon have the estate in efficient order. She is a very intelligent and capable maiden."

The heaviness that clung tenaciously about him was briefly eased by the vicar's low words.

It was true that Beatrice had devoted herself to restoring the house. Not only restoring it, he silently corrected, but preserving the essential beauty and grandeur of the entire estate. It would have been far easier for her to leave the difficult task in the hands of the workmen. Or even his own.

Instead, she had overseen the most tedious details, matching fabrics, carpets, paneling, and fixtures to exacting perfection. Not a speck of dirt was moved without her express approval.

Surely that spoke of some acceptance of her situation, he attempted to comfort himself. Such dedication revealed an emotional commitment whatever her dislike for the Earl of Faulconer.

"Yes, she has already performed no less than a miracle. And, of course, the staff adore her."

"She is very easy to adore," Humbly said softly.

Gabriel resisted the urge to laugh.

Oh, yes, she was all that was adorable.

To everyone but him.

Reaching the wide doorway to the kitchen, Gabriel came to a halt.

"Here we are. I will leave you in Cook's capable hands. I must be off to the fields."

"Certainly." The vicar gave him one last penetrating glance that seemed to reach to his very soul before nodding his head. "I shall see you at dinner, no doubt?"

"Of course."

With a sketchy bow, Gabriel turned and headed directly toward a nearby door.

He had been relieved when he had discovered Beatrice's guest was the simple, elderly vicar.

Now he began to wonder if there wasn't a great deal more to this Mr. Humbly than there appeared to be.

There was something in those eyes.

Something that spoke of a wisdom and perception that could be deucedly disconcerting.

His lips momentarily tightened.

Just what he needed, he thought with a hint of frustration.

Another problem to plague him.

For the first time since becoming Countess of Faulconer, Beatrice carefully attired herself in a satin peach gown and made her way down to the salon.

Perhaps it had been rather childish to insist on eating her meals in splendid isolation. No doubt Gabriel thought it was out of mere spite that she did not join him and Aunt Sarah, as was proper. But in truth she had been unable to bear the thought of sitting at the table pretending that they were simply another married couple.

It smacked too closely of the rosy dreams she had harbored during her all too brief engagement. Dreams of intimate life with the man who had stolen her heart.

Tonight, however, she firmly thrust aside her reluctance and called for her startled maid to help her prepare for the evening ahead. She could hardly hide in her chambers when they possessed a guest. Besides which, she was quite certain the presence of Vicar Humbly would ease the icy atmosphere to at least a bearable level.

Heaven knew, he could not make it worse, she wryly acknowledged.

Standing beside the massive arched window, she was absently tugging upon one of the ribbons on her gown when the door opened and the vicar stepped into the room.

A smile curved her lips as his eyes widened in startled awe. She easily recalled her own amazement when she had first viewed the formal room. Built in an octagon shape, the room was dominated by a vast fireplace with suits of ancient armor guarding the corners and heavy shields hung upon the stone walls. One could almost smell the history and pageantry in the air.

"Oh, my," Humbly murmured as he moved toward Beatrice.

"Quite daunting, is it not?" she demanded in sympathy. "I have not yet decided how to maintain the dignity of the room while adding a bit of comfort."

"A difficult task, indeed." The vicar glanced pointedly toward one of the suits of armor standing at eternal attention. "I feel as if I have been whisked to the past. At any moment I expect a knight to stride across the room and challenge me to a joust."

The mere image of the decidedly rotund vicar perched upon a warhorse and covered in iron was enough to make Beatrice chuckle.

"He would be a very rusty knight," she assured him.

"Yes, we should no doubt hear him squeaking long before he could throw down the gauntlet," Humbly agreed with a smile, then he breathed in deeply, obviously as sensitive as herself to the lingering ghosts in the air. "Such wonderful history in every room."

"It is indeed an ancient holding. I believe that a few of Lord Faulconer's ancestors fought in the Battle of Hastings and were granted these lands for their bravery."

"Goodness. I do hope I can find in the library those books that Lord Faulconer spoke of." Humbly turned to face her with a pleased smile. "Just imagine our sweet Beatrice becoming a part of such an illustrious family."

Beatrice smiled without humor. Oh, yes. How wretchedly clever she had been.

"Not such a feat considering that I bring with me a large fortune." She could not prevent the blunt words from tumbling from her lips. There was little point in dissembling or attempting to pretend that hers had been a love match. Not even this sweet, rather vague gentleman was that blind. "Estates such as Falcon Park are always in desperate need of funds. Or so I have discovered."

Thankfully Mr. Humbly did not appear horrified by her confession. And even more thankfully he did not attempt to deny the fact her fortune had been her primary attraction. Instead, he offered her a glance of gentle understanding.

"You bring with you much more than mere money, Beatrice." He stepped closer, reaching out to grasp her hands in a comforting motion. "You are an intelligent, competent maiden with a sensible manner that will be of far more value to this household than any inheritance. I have already discovered the vast changes you have made for the better, as well as the fact that you are well respected by the servants. They indeed could not say enough good things about their new countess."

Beatrice could not help but be warmed by his kind words. Mr. Humbly had a true gift for making one feel uniquely special. It was, no doubt, why she had so often sought his company when she was young, she acknowledged. Despite her parents' obvious love, Beatrice had always felt awkward and hopelessly plain when in the company of her elegantly beautiful family. It was a relief to be with a gentleman who openly admired her intelligence and even encouraged her eccentric love for mechanical gadgets.

She felt as if she had her own wonderful value as a person when with the vicar.

It was the same way she had felt with Gabriel. At least until she had discovered the truth.

"I am not always sensible, unfortunately," she said as she recalled her foolishness with a wince of pain. "Like all maidens, I can be easily swayed by soft words and shallow charm."

A faint frown formed on his brow at her self-mocking tone. "If you are speaking of following your heart, then you are not supposed to be sensible, my dear. None of us can hope to govern our emotions with our minds. That is what makes it all so delightful."

Delightful?

Gads, the vicar had obviously not had the pleasure of falling in love.

"No, it is not delightful," she retorted, pulling her hands free and moving to stand in the pool of light given by the magnificent gilt metal chandelier. "It is ghastly. Emotions make a person weak and lead them to the most outrageous folly."

There was a small silence before the vicar moved to stand before her, his expression obviously troubled.

"Beatrice, what is it? Are you unhappy here?"

Beatrice swiftly caught back the urge to pour out her troubles like a weepy schoolgirl.

Saints above. This man was her guest. She should be ensuring he was smiling with pleasure, not badgering him with her plight the moment he walked through the door.

She would soon have the reputation of one of those self-obsessed, bitter women who all avoided like the plague.

"Forgive me, Mr. Humbly," she said, summoning a determined smile. "Of course I am not unhappy. I have a great deal to keep me content."

His expression remained troubled. "Content? Hardly the word I would expect from a new bride."

"It is enough," she assured him.

"Beatrice . . ."

The vicar's concerned words were brought to a thankful end as the door was thrust open to reveal a thin, aging woman attired entirely in black. Beatrice smiled wryly as Aunt Sarah paused with astonishment at the sight of a strange gentleman in such proximity. Although a seemingly harmless widow, Aunt Sarah was a master of manipulation, with a tenacity that would put Napoleon to shame.

"Beatrice, my dear, are you joining us for dinner?" she cried, managing to instill a hint of censure for all the evenings Beatrice did not appear. "How lovely."

"Yes, Aunt Sarah. We have a guest," Beatrice retorted in mild tones, far too accustomed to the woman to allow herself to be ruffled. "May I introduce Vicar Humbly? Vicar, this is Lord Faulconer's aunt, Mrs. Quarry."

Like a falcon honing in on its prey, Aunt Sarah swooped across the room and sank her talons into the startled Mr. Humbly's arm.

"A guest. How delightful. And a vicar. Tell me, did your wife travel with you?"

Clearly sensing his sudden danger, Humbly awkwardly cleared his throat. "Ah . . . no. I have never married."

"I see." Aunt Sarah preened with obvious satisfaction. "I myself am a widow. I lost my husband several years ago, poor man. Such a dear, but always so foolish upon his horse. It came as no surprise when he was discovered in a ditch with his neck broken."

Humbly gave a startled cough. "Oh, I am sorry for your loss."

Aunt Sarah heaved a dramatic sigh. "It was a blow. And, of course, becoming a widow at such a young age was a terrible burden. I was forced to become dependent upon my family for their support. I do not know what I would do without dearest Gabriel. Oh, and, of course, Beatrice," she added as a second thought.

Beatrice merely smiled, wickedly enjoying the sight of Humbly struggling to maintain his composure beneath the onslaught of a marriage-mad widow.

"Yes," he at last managed to choke out.

Predictably unaware of the vicar's unease or Beatrice's amusement, Aunt Sarah smiled coyly into Humbly's flushed countenance.

"Not that I haven't had several opportunities to marry again. Several opportunities. But when one reaches our age, Mr. Humbly, we become far more wise and less prone to rash decisions, do we not? I have quite decided that only a comfortable gentleman will do for me now."

Beatrice loudly coughed to cover her burst of laughter at the painfully obvious lure while Humbly cast her a desperate glance.

Really, she had thought the debutantes at Almack's a desperate crew. They had nothing on Aunt Sarah, she acknowledged with poorly concealed amusement.

"Quite understandable," Humbly murmured.

Aunt Sarah batted her lashes. "I suppose that you seek comfort rather than the sparkle of youth?"

"I? Well, I . . ."

The sound of the door opening rescued Humbly from his obvious predicament, although Beatrice discovered herself instinctively stiffening. She knew precisely who she would see as she slowly turned to encounter the hazel gaze of her husband.

Attired in a dark coat and breeches, Gabriel appeared much the same as the first evening she had met him. At that moment she had thought he must be the most handsome gentleman in England with that hair the vibrant color of fall leaves and his hazel eyes gleaming with a ready humor. There had been none of the ennui or sardonic boredom that so marked the men of the *ton*. Instead, he had crackled with a restless energy that had reached across the room and sent a rash of awareness over her skin.

And, of course, there had been that indefinable attraction, she reluctantly conceded. An utterly feminine acknowledgment of his male sensuality that had stirred to life desires she had never before experienced.

Dangerous desires, she thought as a shiver raced through her.

Reaching her side, Gabriel gazed into her wide eyes and offered a potent smile.

"Forgive me for my late arrival. There was some trouble with one of the tenant's cottages." He reached out and audaciously claimed her fingers to lift them to his lips. Beatrice caught her breath, unable to halt the poignant heat that flooded her body. "It is a pleasure to have you join us, my dearest," he murmured.

Beatrice was determined to wrench her hand away. She had made it clear she did not want his false charm or husbandly advances. But even as she told herself that was precisely what she was about to do, she remained gazing into the hazel eyes that seemed to hold a glow of tender warmth. A tenderness that seemed to reach out and touch her battered heart. It was at last the sound of Aunt Sarah loudly clearing her throat that made Beatrice realize what she was doing and with a faint blush she hastily stepped away from her husband.

Gabriel smiled ruefully, but with his usual composure turned to offer Mr. Humbly a half bow. "Vicar, can I offer you a brandy?"

Like a gentleman being offered a reprieve from the gallows, Humbly eagerly detached himself from the tenacious woman at his side.

"Yes, indeed. I should like that very much."

Gabriel's lips twitched as he moved to pour two glasses of brandy from the distant side-table and returned to offer one to the vicar.

"I think you will find this to your taste," he murmured. "If nothing else, my father did manage to keep a respectable cellar."

Humbly took a cautious sip, his eyes widening with pleasure.

"Ah, most fine."

Gabriel gave a pleased nod of his head as he returned to his place at Beatrice's side.

"I trust that you have been made comfortable?"

"Yes, indeed," Humbly was swift to assure him. "Beatrice has taken great care of me."

"The sly child," Aunt Sarah twittered, edging closer to the wary vicar. "She did not breathe a word to me about having a guest. Had I known, I certainly would have made the effort to ensure the vicar's comfort."

Humbly choked on his brandy. "No need to trouble

yourself, Mrs. Quarry. I assure you that Beatrice has seen to all of my needs."

Aunt Sarah pressed her hands to her thin chest. "Trouble? Nonsense. I positively delight in making others comfortable. It is, after all, the duty of poor relatives. Tomorrow I shall see that there is a proper English breakfast and then perhaps later I can show you about the estate."

Humbly shifted his feet, no doubt considering the fine notion of bolting.

"Most kind, I'm sure."

"Oh, it shall be lovely. Gabriel and Beatrice are always so busy that I have grown tediously dull in my own company. I quite look forward to having someone to fuss over."

Perhaps having sent a prayer upward, Humbly was unexpectedly reprieved as the distant sound of a gong echoed through the vaulted chamber.

Taking Beatrice's hand before she could protest, Gabriel laid it upon his arm.

"I believe dinner is ready. Shall we, my dear?" Not waiting for her response, he began to lead her from the room, casting a glance over his shoulder as the vicar reluctantly allowed Aunt Sarah to regain her grasp upon his sleeve. "Do you intend to rescue poor Humbly from Aunt Sarah?" he questioned in low tones.

Beatrice desperately attempted to ignore the clean, warm scent that threatened to wrap about her.

"Perhaps."

"He is looking distinctly harried."

"Aunt Sarah has a tendency to make the stoutest soul appeared harried," she said dryly.

Their gazes briefly met in companionable amusement. It was a glance they had shared numerous times during their courtship. A glance that said they understood precisely what the other was thinking without saying a word.

"Yes, indeed," he said softly. "I should dislike, however, for the vicar to be run off too swiftly. It is obvious that you enjoy his company."

Beatrice forced her gaze toward the shadowed hall, wishing her heart would steady its erratic beat.

"I do. Mr. Humbly is very kind and far more clever than one would suspect by his vague manner."

Gabriel gave a dry laugh. "I had already suspected as much. Does it matter?"

She unconsciously tightened her fingers upon his arm. "He is bound to realize that all is not well between us."

"He would not need to be particularly clever to deduce that, my dear. It is hardly a secret."

"No, I suppose not."

A thick silence descended, broken only by the swish of her satin skirts and the distant chatter flowing from Aunt Sarah. Then Gabriel reached up to cover her fingers with his hand.

"There is a simple solution to your dilemma, Beatrice," he said in odd tones.

"Really? And what is that?"

"Make this marriage real."

Beatrice stumbled as a rash of fear and excitement churned through her stomach.

"It is real."

"No, it is no more than a shallow imitation," he said lowly.

Her gaze abruptly lifted to stab him with a glittering glare. "Do you mean that you wish for me to allow you into my bed?"

The hazel eyes briefly flared with what might have been desire before he was drawing in a deep breath.

"It would certainly be a beginning, but that is not all I speak of."

Disconcerted more by the clamoring ache deep within her than his smooth offer, Beatrice gave a sharp shake of her head.

No. She did not want to desire Gabriel.

Not now.

"No."

His hand briefly tightened on her hand, then he was forcing a smile to his lips.

"Then we shall simply have to endure the undoubted curiosity of the vicar, will we not?"

Three

Gabriel polished off his third plate of ham, eggs, and toast with a satisfied sigh.

Thank God Beatrice had discovered such a treasure in the kitchen, he acknowledged.

Although a slender gentleman, he had always possessed a hearty appetite, and the long hours in the fields only sharpened his need for plentiful food.

The mere thought of fields brought a small groan to his lips.

Lud, he ached from head to toe. Not even the years on the battlefield had prepared him for the backbreaking work of cutting hay, repairing fences, thatching cottages, and restoring the outbuildings. His hands were callused, his back so sore he could barely move, and his feet blistered by the hours of wading through mud, hay, and gravel.

So much for the image of a gentleman of leisure, he sighed. The only leisure he enjoyed was when he managed to stumble to his bed and pass out from sheer exhaustion.

Of course, for all his aches and pains, he could not deny a sense of growing satisfaction. Much to his surprise, he discovered he enjoyed seeing the direct results of his labor. It was one thing to watch the tenants laboring in the fields or commanding workmen to repair the ravaged barns and outbuildings. It was quite another to climb upon a cottage and realize his hours of labor would ensure a family slept dry in their beds that evening.

Being so directly involved in the estate was weaving a bond with the land and people that would never have developed while sitting in an office or speaking with his steward. How could a man remain immune when he could see the immediate results of his efforts with his own eyes?

A pity hard work alone could not have saved Falcon Park, he thought with an uncomfortable pang.

He could have taken pure pride in reclaiming his heritage had he been able to save it with his own hands. As it was, he knew that his pleasure in his estate would always be shadowed by Beatrice's sadness.

Almost as if his unwelcome thought had conjured the presence of his bride, Beatrice swept into the room, coming to an abrupt halt at the sight of his lone form at the breakfast table.

She had clearly just left her chambers, as her soft cinnamon gown was not yet marred with dirt and her ribbons remained intact. Her honey curls, however, were already tenaciously slipping from the knot atop her head to play about her cheeks in a charmingly haphazard manner.

Rising to his feet, he watched in wry resignation as she hovered close to the door. No doubt considering the best means of escaping, he acknowledged.

"Good morning, my dear," he murmured in determined tones.

More or less trapped for the moment, Beatrice absently plucked at the ribbon tied beneath the high waist of her gown.

"Mr. Humbly is not yet down?"

"Oh, yes. He has already eaten and been swept off by a very determined Aunt Sarah."

"Oh."

A small silence fell before Gabriel waved a hand toward the table.

"Will you not join me?"

She glanced over her shoulder, perhaps hoping for inspiration, or at least a timely reprieve.

"I am not really hungry," she at last said weakly.

Gabriel clenched his hands in frustration. "Oh, for goodness' sake, have a seat, Beatrice. I am not about to pounce in the middle of the breakfast room."

She flushed at his sharp tone. "You need not snap at me."

"Forgive me, but I fear the knowledge that my wife cannot bear to be in my presence occasionally strikes a nerve."

"I simply prefer to avoid our unpleasant squabbles," she protested in stiff tones.

Gabriel did not believe her.

Oh, not that she disliked the prickly tension between them. No one could wish to be forever at odds with another.

But there was more to her hurried retreats and icy demeanor than mere dislike, he slowly acknowledged. There was a hint of wariness that made him wonder precisely what she was hiding behind her icy defenses.

"Then shall we make an effort to avoid such unpleasantness?" he questioned in cautious tones. "With Mr. Humbly staying at Falcon Park we are destined to be spending at least some time together. Surely it would be better for all if we could at least manage to be polite to each other?"

There was a pause before Beatrice gave a restless shrug at his obviously sensible suggestion.

"I shall make the attempt."

Emboldened by her agreement, Gabriel offered a faint smile. "It was once not such an effort. Do you recall the night we slipped from the Dunby ball and strolled through the gardens?"

He could see her visibly stiffen, but thankfully she did not scurry away as he had feared she might.

"I recall that it was cold."

He moved around the table, careful not to make any sudden movements, as if she were some wary prey he was stalking.

"We walked for nearly an hour before we returned to the house. We had no difficulty getting along that evening."

"Of course not. I foolishly thought that you desired to be with me because you genuinely liked me. Did it amuse you to pretend an interest in my childish babblings?"

His heart flinched at her rapier-edged words. Lud, but she knew how to strike where it hurt the most.

"Stop it, Beatrice," he said in low tones. "I never pretended when I was with you. I have always liked and respected you."

She waved aside his words with patent disbelief. "I do have one question, my lord."

Gabriel gritted his teeth at her refusal to even consider the notion his emotions had been sincere.

"Gabriel."

She blinked in confusion. "What?"

"My name is Gabriel. As your husband, I believe that I have the right to at least have you use my proper name."

"Right?"

"Yes. God knows I ask nothing else."

A faint color stained her cheeks at his deliberate words. "If you insist."

"I believe I must," he commanded. "Now, what is the question?"

There was a moment's pause before she tilted her chin to regard him with a steady gaze.

"Why me?"

Gabriel frowned. "I beg your pardon?"

"Why me?" she repeated in tight tones. "The *ton* is littered with heiresses. Not all inheritences as large as mine, but certainly enough for your needs. Was it because you knew I was not likely to receive an offer from another?"

Gabriel suddenly felt as if he had been catapulted back onto the battlefield.

Blast it all.

She had to know there was no way to answer the danger-fraught question without wounding her further.

Disaster loomed all about him.

"For God's sake, Beatrice," he muttered.

"Will you not answer me?"

"What is the point of this discussion now?"

An indefinable emotion rippled over her pale features. "Because I wish to know."

"Very well." He unconsciously squared his shoulders. "I chose you because you professed a preference for living in the country. I knew the estate would demand a great deal of my time to save it from disaster, and I could not pander to a woman who preferred to be gadding about London."

Her gaze never wavered. "And it had nothing to do with the fact that I had no other suitors who might warn me of your true intentions?"

Gabriel heaved a harsh sigh, raking a hand through his russet hair. "You demand your pound of flesh, do you not, my dear?"

"I simply wish the truth between us for a change."

Gabriel searched the strong features, wondering why she was suddenly so determined to insist upon a conversation she had so diligently avoided for weeks.

Did she truly desire to clear the air between them? Or was she simply searching for further cause to fan the flames of her self-righteous anger?

He was no doubt damned either way, he ruefully told himself.

"Then, yes," he reluctantly conceded. "It suited my purpose not to battle my way past dozens of admirers. I am a soldier, not a practiced flirt. I could not fool myself that I was capable of dazzling any woman with my wit and charm. My only hope was discovering a maiden who preferred a plainspoken gentleman to a well-versed rake."

Her hands clutched at the skirt of her gown, crushing the soft fabric beyond repair.

"How delighted you must have been to discover an awkward, plain maiden who hadn't the least notion of how to play the games of flirtation."

Gabriel moved forward to grasp her shoulders in a tight grasp. Dash it all. She could brand him as the devil, but he would not have her mocking her own special qualities.

"You are not awkward or plain, but I was pleased that you were not a shallow flirt. I genuinely thought with your practical nature and dislike for society you would enjoy your life at Falcon Park." His lips twisted in a humorless smile. "Obviously I vastly overrated the shabby charm of my estate."

Her gaze abruptly dropped. He was well aware that she could not deny any affection for Falcon Park. Not when she poured such passion into having it restored.

A passion he deeply envied.

"This has nothing to do with Falcon Park, as you well know."

His fingers moved to absently brush back a honey curl. Her hair was soft with a beguiling scent of honeysuckle. He suddenly longed to plunge his fingers into those thick curls and tumble them about her shoulders.

"So, it is my own charms you find so sadly lacking," he said in an effort to distract himself. Only the Lord above knew what would happen if he gave into his masculine impulse. A bloody nose, most likely. "I am wounded, my dear."

"I see you find this a matter for jest," she accused in husky tones.

Gabriel's fingers moved to lightly cup her chin and tugged her face upward. Having her so close was reminding him far too forcibly of the few occasions she had readily allowed him to hold her in his arms. At the time he had gloried in the swift desire he could feel running through her body. He had known that their marriage bed would be one of utter delight for both of them.

Unwelcome stirrings deep within him made Gabriel clench his teeth.

No.

He had no desire for a bloody nose directly after breakfast.

"No, I find nothing particularly amusing about being tied to a woman who treats me as if I am the latest plague," he retorted.

The amber eyes abruptly flared. "How did you expect me to react when I discovered the truth?"

"I had hoped you would trust me enough to realize I would never do anything to hurt you."

"But you did hurt me, Gabriel." Without warning she stepped from his touch, her expression unforgiving.

"And I will never be so foolish as to trust you again. Excuse me, I must rescue poor Mr. Humbly from Aunt Sarah."

Gabriel could do nothing as she turned and hurried away.

Nothing but curse the fate that had taken his father's yacht and landed him with a bankrupt estate, a hundred starving tenants, and a wife who wished him in Hades.

Being Earl of Faulconer was certainly not all that it was cracked up to be.

Vicar Humbly had endured many trials during his lifetime.

During his childhood he had not only been poor, but already plump enough to be the focus of the neighborhood children's teasing.

He had been emotionally blackmailed into becoming a vicar by his father when he desired to become a dashing soldier.

He had lost his true love when she had been forced to wed for money.

He had endured years of abuse from the crusty old squire who believed he was appointed by God to make Vicar Humbly's life miserable.

But for all the tribulations he had faced and overcome, nothing had prepared him for Mrs. Quarry.

For nearly an hour he had sought to extract himself from her tenacious clutches.

He had lagged far behind her brisk pace. He had complained of his feet aching. He had even briefly pretended to be struck by a pang in his stomach until the widow had made it clear she intended to see him to his chambers and personally oversee his recovery.

With a shudder Humbly trailed his way behind the woman as they made their way down the hall.

Dear heavens, he had traveled to Derbyshire to help sweet Beatrice, not to be tortured by a marriage-mad widow. Shouldn't such a good deed be rewarded, not punished?

It appeared not, as the shrill voice of Mrs. Quarry floated endlessly through the musty air and Humbly gazed longingly out the arched windows at the inviting sunlight outside.

He could leap, he acknowledged wryly. Goodness knew that a broken leg or two would be a small price to pay for blessed freedom.

Perhaps at last hearing his fervent prayers for salvation, God softened his heart toward his poor servant and Humbly watched in desperate relief as Beatrice suddenly stepped in the hallway like an angel from above.

The vicar could quite willingly have kissed her there and then.

"Mr. Humbly." She greeted him with a smile.

Scurrying toward her with indecent haste, Humbly reached out to grasp her hand.

"Beatrice, my dear."

"I trust I am not interrupting?" she demanded with a knowing glance at his flushed companion.

"No, no. Not at all. Delighted to see you."

"I thought perhaps you would wish to join me this morning. There is a gentleman with a particularly interesting device."

"Yes, indeed," he breathed in relief. "I cannot conceive of anything I would enjoy more."

Suddenly realizing she was about to lose her captive, Mrs. Quarry rushed toward them with an anxious expression.

"But, Mr. Humbly, we were just about to view the gardens."

"Perhaps later, Mrs. Quarry," he said in vague tones.

"Surely you cannot be interested in those horrid inventions," she protested with a sweet voice that managed to scrap a gentleman's nerves with hair-raising effect. "So noisy and unpleasant."

"I am very interested in all innovations. They are such an intriguing glimpse of the future."

A hint of annoyance rippled over the thin face before the widow forced a smile back to her narrow lips.

"How very romantic you make them sound, Mr. Humbly. I can tell you possess the soul of a poet."

Humbly gave a choked cough. "Oh, no. I am nothing more than a plodding vicar with few talents and a desire for nothing more romantic than simple peace at my small cottage."

The widow batted her lashes. "Now, now. There is no need to be so modest. A plodding vicar, indeed."

"Come along, Mr. Humbly." Beatrice thankfully rushed to the rescue. "We should not be late for our appointment."

Humbly was more than eager to allow himself to be led down the hall and away from the persistent Mrs. Quarry. A glance at his companion's countenance, however, made him give a loud harrumph.

"Do you find something amusing, Beatrice?"

She allowed the laughter she had valiantly restrained to echo through the vaulted hall.

"I was just thinking that you will have to be far more blunt if you wish to distract Aunt Sarah from her pursuit."

Humbly grimaced. "She is a very determined lady."

"Very determined." Beatrice steered them toward a narrow flight of stairs that led toward the back terrace.

"You will have to be upon your toes if you desire to avoid becoming entangled in her web."

The mere thought was enough to make the vicar's stomach roll in an alarming fashion.

"Dear heavens. She must be very desperate to turn her attentions to a poor, aging vicar."

Beatrice flashed him a charming smile. "Nonsense. I would say she possesses excellent taste. What woman would not desire a gentleman who is so kind and gentle?"

Humbly firmly put the woman from his mind. Mrs. Quarry and her hunt for a husband thankfully had nothing to do with his visit to Derbyshire.

"And is that what you searched for in a husband, my dear?" he inquired in deliberately light tones.

Her steps momentarily faltered before Beatrice grasped the wooden railing and continued down the stairs.

"That was my hope, certainly."

"But Lord Faulconer is not kind or gentle? Does he abuse you, Beatrice?"

She flashed him a satisfyingly shocked glance. "Of course not."

"But he is not what you had hoped him to be?"

Her lips twisted. "You are very perceptive."

"It does not take much perception to realize you are not happy, my dear."

"I suppose not." She grimaced ruefully. "I have never been good at hiding my feelings."

They reached the bottom of the stairs and Humbly placed a hand on Beatrice's arm to bring her to a halt. His heart ached to see the barely hidden wounds in her beautiful eyes.

"What is it, Beatrice?"

She hesitated, no doubt considering whether he would be satisfied with a flippant response. But his expression of gentle determination must have warned her that he was not to be swayed, as she heaved a resigned sigh.

"When I first met Lord Faulconer I thought him different from the other gentlemen of the *ton,*" she at last said in tones so low they were barely audible. "He did not attempt to turn my head with absurd claims of beauty I obviously do not possess, nor seek to lure me into a compromising situation as so many fortune hunters had attempted before. Instead, he truly appeared interested in my odd fancies and not at all put off by my lack of female talents."

"He seems to be a very wise gentleman," Humbly complimented with a smile.

She wrapped her arms about her waist in an unwittingly protective manner.

"Wise enough to realize that I would not be fooled by the sort of flirtations most women prefer. Instead, he won my trust by pretending to be my friend."

Having seen the painful longing in Lord Faulconer's eyes, Humbly gave a slow shake of his head.

"Pretending? Are you certain, Beatrice?"

She gave a short, humorless laugh. "Look about you, Mr. Humbly. Falcon Park was on the threshold of tumbling into obscurity. Lord Faulconer's only hope in saving the estate was to wed for money. A great deal of money."

"Well, many of the *ton* choose their spouses for reasons other than love," Humbly pointed out in reasonable tones. "That does not mean he is not your friend."

A flare of pain hardened her features. It was obvious she felt betrayed by the man who had won her trust.

"If he had been my friend, he would have told me from the beginning he was seeking an heiress. The fact that he deliberately allowed me to believe he was well situated proves that he had no concern for my feelings."

Humbly could easily sympathize with the poor girl.

He did not doubt she had been wounded, not only by Lord Faulconer's treachery, but even more so by the realization that she had been betrayed by her own heart.

Had Lord Faulconer forced her into marriage through blackmail or compromise she would have been furious. But to have stolen her heart . . . well, it was a sin that would not easily be forgiven.

Still, Humbly could not find it in his mind to wholly condemn Lord Faulconer. He had been wrong to mislead Beatrice. Especially when he must have sensed her heart was involved. But the burdens he had been so unexpectedly forced to shoulder could not have been easy to bear. And deep within him Humbly believed that he did care for Beatrice. Perhaps far more than either realized.

"And if he told you the truth from the beginning?" he asked softly.

She gave a restless shrug. "I do not know."

"Beatrice." He moved his hand to grasp her cold fingers. "If you are so unhappy here, why do you not return to Surrey? Your parents would be pleased to have you home."

She was giving a firm shake of her head before he even finished.

"No one forced me to wed Lord Faulconer. It was a mistake I made on my own. I will not have my family fretting over me."

There was a sharp edge in her voice that made Humbly study her with a hint of curiosity.

"Are you sure that is the only reason?"

"What do you mean?"

Humbly chose his words with care. He sensed that beneath her bitter anger still lurked a great deal of feeling for her husband, but he also realized she would be horrified if he were to suggest such a notion.

He would have to somehow nudge her into accepting her love in her own fashion.

"It seems that you have been deeply hurt by your husband. But it also occurs to me that you have not entirely given up hope on this marriage. You would not be so determined to punish Lord Faulconer if you did not intend to forgive him eventually."

Four

Beatrice regarded the vicar with undisguised shock.

Obviously Mr. Humbly was becoming daft in his old age, she told herself as she shifted in unease. Or the long journey had addled his wits.

"That is absurd."

"Is it?" Humbly demanded in mild tones.

"Yes, I have no desire to punish Lord Faulconer."

The gray brows lifted with evident disbelief at her fierce words.

"Then you must be a remarkable young woman. Few ladies would be so sensible. It is human nature to wish to strike back at those who have wounded us. Even the kindest dog will snap when it has been hurt."

She widened her eyes. "So you believe I am a dog snapping at my captor?"

He gently patted her hand. "I think you a woman who is feeling betrayed and wishing to ease your pain in the only manner that is offered. I do not judge you, Beatrice. In truth, I would do precisely the same thing in your position."

Unnerved by his determined accusations, Beatrice turned to pace across the small foyer. He made her sound like a petulant child. Or, worse, a vindictive harpy who cared only for hurting others.

Could he not understand the pain she was enduring?

That she was still attempting to reconcile herself to the knowledge her hopes and dreams for a marriage based on love were forever destroyed?

"It is not a matter of punishment," she at last retorted, nearly tugging the ribbon from the neckline of her gown. "I am merely furious at having been so easily duped."

She could hear him move to stand behind her stiff form. "And hoping to make Lord Faulconer regret his deceit?"

She felt a thrust of annoyance. Gads, he was as tenacious as Aunt Sarah.

"Yes, I suppose," she reluctantly conceded.

The vicar placed a comforting hand upon her shoulder. "I believe he does sincerely regret hurting you, Beatrice."

She briefly closed her eyes as the pain shuddered through her. Saints above. She had thought Humbly her friend. How could he sympathize with Gabriel?

"He regrets the fact that I discovered the truth of this marriage and have failed to be the adoring, dutiful wife that he expected."

There was a startled silence, then without warning Mr. Humbly's laughter rang through the air.

"Oh, Beatrice."

Thoroughly offended at his obvious lack of concern for her delicate sensibilities, she turned to regard him with a frown.

"It is hardly amusing, Vicar."

"The thought of you ever being an adoring, dutiful wife is certainly amusing, my dear," he retorted without the faintest hint of apology. "You are far too intelligent and strong-willed to ever be the sort of biddable wife that you seem to think Lord Faulconer would prefer."

Her flare of annoyance faded as her own sense of

humor was restored. It was true she had never pretended to be a milk and toast debutant. Her temperament was not suited to constantly giving sway to another.

"You make me sound a shrew," she forced herself to protest.

"No, no." He gave a shake of his head. "Just a very strong woman who knows her own mind."

Her lips twitched. "Perhaps."

"So had Lord Faulconer desired a meek wife, why did he not chose one? I daresay you were not the only heiress in all of England."

Beatrice abruptly recalled her conversation with Gabriel only moments before. She was still uncertain as to why she had suddenly pressed for his confession. She had refused to discuss their marriage from the moment she had discovered the truth of why he had wed her. But somehow it had seemed important to hear the words from his own lips.

Perhaps to bolster her faltering anger, a treacherous voice whispered in the back of her mind.

It was a voice she swiftly stifled.

No.

It was just as she had said. It was time for honesty between them.

"He chose me because I prefer the country and because I had no other suitors he needed to battle for my attention."

Humbly gave a click of his tongue. "Perhaps those were the initial reasons he sought you out, but I believe he chose you for yourself."

She gave a rueful shake of her head. "That is only because you are good and kind and can never see anything but good in others."

"I am not so naive that I do not see a gentleman who regards his wife with longing."

Beatrice froze.

Longing?

No gentleman had ever gazed at her with longing.

Least of all her husband.

"You are mistaken, Mr. Humbly," she said in flat tones. "Lord Faulconer might desire a wife who is comfortable and willing to provide him with heirs, but he does not long for me."

As if sensing he had struck where she was most vulnerable, Humbly offered a rather sad smile. "If you insist. Tell me, Beatrice, do you intend to remain angry forever?"

A cold chill inched down her spine. She rarely allowed herself to think of the future.

"You think that I should simply put aside the fact that I was gulled by a fortune hunter?" she demanded.

He smiled gently. "I think that you should consider the notion that you have a goodly number of years to live with Lord Faulconer. How you choose to spend those days is in your hands."

She flinched at his direct hit. When she had thought Gabriel her friend their days together did not seem nearly long enough. She had imagined them side by side as they built a life together. Each day filled with love and laughter as they created a family that would surround them with happiness.

It had all been so simple.

Now Mr. Humbly was forcing her to consider the future as it was, not as she had dreamed it would be.

She gave a sharp shake of her head, not yet prepared to consider his challenging words.

Not yet.

"We must go," she stated in firm tones.

Humbly reached out to pat her hand. "Beatrice, at

least think upon what I have said. I believe you could be happy at Falcon Park if you chose to."

Beatrice merely moved to the door and stepped onto the back terrace. Mr. Humbly simply did not understand, she thought with an inner sigh.

Attempting to thrust aside the disturbing conversation, Beatrice briskly crossed the terrace and headed toward the stable yard, where she generally viewed the inventions.

She had enough to occupy herself without brooding upon the vague future, she assured herself.

As if to prove her point, she spotted her thin, stoically efficient secretary whom she had hired when she had first arrived at Falcon Park. Beatrice allowed a smile to curve her lips. This was her favorite part of her day, and for once the elusive spring sunlight had struggled from the clouds to provide a welcome warmth. More often than not she was chilled and thoroughly drenched before she had concluded her business.

"Mr. Eaton, what do you have for me today?"

A rare smile touched the narrow countenance. "A most fascinating machine, Lady Falconer," he said as he led her toward a bulky gentleman who was building a fire beneath a large barrel that had been drilled with holes and set upon two poles so that it could be rotated. "I think you will be intrigued."

Beatrice moved to study the large man who was busily lifting a lid he had cut into the barrel and stuffing a number of wet rags into the opening. He then closed the lid and reached for a handle that had been attached to the barrel and began turning it at a brisk pace.

For nearly twenty minutes she watched in silence as he continued to turn the barrel over the flames, until at last the man halted and pulled out the rags. He handed them to Beatrice with a triumphant smile.

With delight Beatrice discovered the material completely dry. No small feat for rags that had been dripping with water.

Circling the barrel, she asked several questions of the eager inventor, as much to determine his character and ambition as to discover more of his machine. Then, requesting Mr. Eaton to take his name and address, she motioned to Mr. Humbly that she was prepared to return to the house.

He readily joined her, his sherry eyes glowing with excitement.

"Truly fascinating," he breathed as they angled toward the terrace. "A most remarkable machine, do you not think, my dear?"

Beatrice gave a slow nod of her head, her swift mind already sorting through the various flaws of the invention.

"I see possibilities. There are several problems with the design, however."

Humbly sent her a surprised glance. "Really? What problems?"

Beatrice wrinkled her brow in thought. "Well, to begin with, I do not suppose many servants would prefer to stand over a hot fire, turning the barrel, when they can hang up the clothes and allow nature to take its course."

"Yes, I suppose that is true enough," Humbly slowly agreed.

"And, of course, there is the problem of protecting the drying clothes from the smell of smoke." She gave a faint grimace at the acrid scent that clung to her own gown. "It is not an aroma that anyone would enjoy."

"Oh." Humbly's expression dimmed, rather like a small child who discovered his new toy was not as shiny as he had thought. "I had not considered the smoke."

Beatrice smiled indulgently. It was a pleasure to have

someone with her who became as intrigued by inventions as herself.

"Still, there is much to consider," she assured him. "The notion of drying clothes within an hour or less rather than taking an entire day has much to recommend it. Yes, I shall definitely give it some thought."

They traveled some distance before Beatrice turned her head to discover the vicar regarding her in a speculative manner.

"My dear, you amaze me," he at last said with a smile.

She gave a startled blink. "Why?"

He lifted his pudgy hands. "Within moments you have been able to precisely determine the strengths and weaknesses of that machine. Just as your grandfather was able to do."

Beatrice could not prevent the warm flood of pleasure at his words. There were few things that pleased her more than being compared to the grandfather she had adored.

"That is hardly amazing," she forced herself to retort modestly. "It is simply a matter of being practical."

"No. It is a gift," he argued in firm tones. "You should be quite proud."

She smiled at his gentle kindness, then a movement in the distant garden caught her eye. She came to an abrupt halt.

"Oh."

Stopping beside her, Mr. Humbly gave a lift of his brows. "What is it?"

"I believe I glimpsed Aunt Sarah just beyond the hedge," she warned.

Humbly shuddered. "Egads."

She flashed him a knowing glance. "If you wish to return to your chambers, you can slip through the side door."

He heaved a relieved sigh. "Yes, indeed. Thank you, my dear."

"I must meet with the architect, but I should be free in an hour or so. Shall we meet in the library?"

"A lovely notion." He offered her a hasty bow. "Until then."

Before continuing her path to the terrace, Beatrice watched Humbly scurry away.

Poor man, she silently sympathized. Having been pursued for years by desperate gentlemen, she knew precisely how he felt. There was nothing pleasant about being a fox among hounds.

She supposed that she should at least be thankful to Gabriel for relieving her of such unpleasantness, she wryly conceded.

She need never worry about fortune hunters again.

Carefully comparing the crimson-figured damask she had ordered from London with the faded fabric taken from the dining room chairs, Beatrice gave a decisive nod of her head.

"I believe this will do very well," she announced.

"Yes, my lady. The craftsmen have done an excellent job in matching the pattern," the large, rather somber architect retorted.

"When will the paneling be returned?"

"Later in the week, although I will travel to London myself to collect the carpets and tapestries. I do not trust the artisans to restore them properly without supervision."

Beatrice hid a smile. Although she could be exacting in her demands, she knew this gentleman was next to impossible to please. The poor artist restoring the medieval joust scene painted above the door had come to her on several occasions claiming he could not work beneath such critical demands.

"Very good. That will be all for today."

"Yes, Lady Faulconer."

With a bow the architect smoothly withdrew from the formal dining room and Beatrice wandered toward the Breccia marble chimneypiece. At the moment the room appeared starkly empty. Only the fan-vaulted ceiling and stained glass windows had escaped the ruthless demolition that had been necessary to repair the years of damage.

In her mind's eye, however, she could envision the grandeur of the room once it was complete.

She knew precisely where each chair, each candelabrum, and each tapestry would be placed. She had even sent the ancient clock and silver tea service to London to be repaired. It would soon be returned precisely as it had been before the decline of the Faulconer fortune.

Without the drafts and leaking casements, she acknowledged wryly.

Knowing she should return to her chambers and change the gown now streaked with soot and dust, Beatrice turned about only to catch her breath at the sight of Gabriel leaning against the door frame, regarding her with a brooding gaze.

As she stiffened in surprise, he slowly pushed himself away from the door and strolled to the center of the room.

"Quite a change," he said with a faint smile.

Beatrice clasped her hands together, experiencing that wary unease she always felt when her husband was near.

"I fear that it was necessary to strip the room bare before it could be restored."

"I am not complaining," he retorted in mild tones, his

gaze traveling over the bare walls and clutter of ladders and tools. "The last occasion I was in this room my father was hosting a drunken party and I was nearly strung from the chandelier when I refused to allow one of the guests to pile the chairs onto the fire when they ran out of firewood."

Beatrice felt a stab of surprise at his wry words. Gabriel rarely discussed his childhood, although she had already surmised that it had been less than idyllic. To have watched his father and brother deliberately destroying their inheritance must have been painfully frustrating.

"It could not have been very comfortable for you to stay here."

He glanced at her in surprise, as if caught off guard by her hint of compassion.

"It was damnable," he agreed slowly, the hazel eyes somber. "Unlike my father and brother, I took no enjoyment from endless pursuits of pleasure and their coarse friends. I found it inconceivable that they would squander their income upon cards and drink while the roof threatened to crumble down upon their heads."

Beatrice could not halt a reluctant tug of understanding. She knew precisely what it felt like to be among those who were so utterly dissimilar that they might be from two separate lands.

"Very frustrating, no doubt," she murmured.

"Yes." He gave a wry grimace. "Although to be fair, I was equally frustrating to my father. He often mourned that he must have been cuckolded, since no son of his could prefer books to the hunt or show such an utter lack of interest in pursuing every maid who passed through the door."

Beatrice paused, knowing she should leave the room. There was something suddenly very vulnerable about Gabriel as he revealed his unhappy childhood. A vulnerability that threatened to melt the ice encasing her heart.

Her feet did not move, however, and instead she discovered herself probing even deeper.

"That is why you bought a commission?"

He gave an elegant lift of one shoulder. "One of the reasons. More than anything, it was impossible to watch as the tenants and servants began to suffer beneath my father's neglect. Crumbling roofs were despicable enough. Allowing those who depend upon you to starve was more than I could bear."

"So you chose to fight Napoleon instead," she said, wondering what her life might have been had she possessed the means of leaving her home without stepping into marriage.

He gave a short laugh. "It seemed safer than remaining and throttling my family. It is a choice I deeply regret, however."

Her gaze narrowed. "Why?"

"Had I remained, I might have been able to put at least some restraint upon my father. Or at least have hidden a few of the more valuable jewels so that I could help those who had nothing," he explained, unable to hide his self-disgust. "Instead, I walked away and washed my hands of Falcon Park. It was by far the easier path."

Without thinking, she lifted her hands to indicate the barren room. It had taken more than a handful of years to reduce Falcon Park to its current state of neglect.

"Do you truly believe that had you been here you could have prevented this?"

"I would at least have the satisfaction of knowing I tried," he said, more to himself than her. Then he forced a smile to his lips. "Forgive me, Beatrice. I did not come here to pour out my troubles."

The sharp stab of disappointment at his sudden retreat made Beatrice sternly chastise her foolishness. She did not want to feel pity for Gabriel's difficult past. Or to consider the notion he had clearly been in desperate straits to save Falcon Park. And certainly she did not want to feel that odd bond that had drawn her to him in the first place.

With an effort she feigned a hint of indifference. He must not realize just how easily he could slip beneath her defenses.

"Is there something you need?"

An indefinable emotion briefly darkened the hazel eyes before he was giving a shrug.

"As much as I dislike adding to your burdens, I fear that I should warn you that a battle appears to be brewing in the garden between the workmen and Chalfrey. Something about a tree that was seemingly planted by the first Lady Faulconer in honor of the King."

"Not again." Beatrice sighed in exasperation. The cantankerous Chalfrey was truly going to drive her batty. "I thought by returning the family gardener to his position he would be eager to help restore the grounds. Instead, he adamantly insists that every rock and tree is somehow sacred to the Faulconer family."

"Do you wish me to speak with him?" Gabriel offered. "Chalfrey can be a stubborn, ill-tempered old brute."

Beatrice gave a shake of her head. The staff was now her responsibility as well as Gabriel's, and she knew it was important to establish her authority. Even if it meant a brangle with the aggravating gardener.

"No, I will deal with him. I wish to make it very clear that the work I have ordered will proceed with or without his approval."

"Even if it means cutting down trees planted in honor of kings?" he lightly teased.

She stilled, eyeing him in a wary fashion. "Do you disapprove?"

"Of course not," he swiftly reassured her, moving to stand far too close for her peace of mind. "Over the past centuries the gardens have been altered on several occasions. I doubt any of the original trees still stand. Besides, if Prinny has not yet come to admire his family's tree, I doubt if he will do so in the near future."

Beatrice barely heard his soothing words. Instead, she was nearly consumed by the prickling awareness that swept through her body. How many nights had she dreamed of being held in his strong arms? Of having his lips pressed to her own as he seduced a wicked excitement deep with in her?

A shiver shook her form as a rash of goose bumps feathered over her skin.

"I should speak with Chalfrey," she blurted out, moving hastily to put some much-needed distance between them. Her haste, however, was her undoing, and even as she attempted to step past him, her foot caught in the hem of her gown and she was lunging forward. "Oh."

"Careful." With annoying ease, he managed to catch her and sweep her closer to the disturbing heat of his body. "Are you all right?"

A dark flush stained her cheeks. As much for the betraying pleasure at being held so close to him as for embarrassment at her clumsiness.

"Yes, so stupid of me," she muttered, glaring down at her torn hem in exasperation. "I do not know how I manage to destroy every gown I put on."

Without warning, his hand moved to grasp her chin and tilted her face up to meet his stern gaze.

"Do not."

She gave a startled blink. "What?"

"I have always admired the fact that you do not twitter over your appearance."

"It would do little good if I did," she said dryly.

His fingers moved to trace a searing path over her cheek. "Beatrice, your beauty has always come from within you. Your habit of tossing yourself wholeheartedly into whatever you are doing. Your ability to make life better for those about you, and your kindness to those in need. Such qualities are far more important than fripperies."

Her heart came to a full, painful stop at his soft words. She had sworn she would not be swayed by this man again. He had effectively proven he was not to be trusted. But even as she sought to pull away she found herself lost in the dark hazel gaze.

"Gabriel?"

His lips tilted at her bewildered tone. "Yes, Beatrice?"

"I should go."

"Must you?" he demanded.

Keeping their gazes locked, he slowly lowered his head. There was no mistaking the fact he was about to kiss her, but while a warning voice insisted that she pull away, Beatrice was unable to move. It was as if a spell had been cast over her, making it impossible to move so much as a muscle. And then his mouth was claiming her own in a soft, achingly tender kiss. All thought of protest fled as the cascade of sensations shimmered through her. Saints above, it had been so long. So very long since he had made her tremble with desire.

"Oh, Beatrice, I've missed holding you in my arms," he murmured as he stroked his lips over her cheek. "You taste sweet, so sweet."

For a crazed moment Beatrice leaned against the hard heat of his body, reveling in the desire stirring to life between them. It had always been like this for her.

Gabriel had only to touch her to make her heart falter and her blood race. It was a dizzying, magical feeling.

The seeking lips found the curve of her neck and began to nibble their way downward. His hands splayed across her back, the heat of his skin burning through the fabric of her gown.

She wanted the moment to last forever.

To be held and caressed as if he truly loved her . . .

The thought passed through her foggy mind at the same moment she was abruptly wrenching from his grasp.

No.

He did not love her.

He had never loved her.

Horrified at the ease in which she had allowed herself to be bewitched, Beatrice gave a choked cry, then, pressing a hand to her aching lips, she fled from the room.

Dear heavens.

She had just exposed what she had sworn never to reveal, she acknowledged as tears stung her eyes.

She had just allowed him to realize he could crash through her defenses with a single touch.

Five

Gabriel watched with a jaundiced gaze as his aunt Sarah excused herself from the table. Under the best of circumstances, the woman's constant prattle was annoying. When he was in a foul mood, it was nearly impossible to bear.

Sipping deeply of the port that had been silently placed upon the table, he scowled at the closing door. It did not help that he knew precisely what had affected his mood, he acknowledged sourly. It was what affected his mood every day.

Beatrice.

His teeth clenched as he thought of his exasperating wife.

He had been so certain that they had made progress on this day.

Not only had they managed a conversation free of the usual barbs and heated accusations, but he had actually held her in his arms.

A shaft of blazing need shot through him as he remembered the feel of her soft curves pressed to his own. He had told himself that it was mere imagination that made him recall her kisses with such a deep longing. Surely kisses were kisses no matter who the woman? But the moment his mouth had touched her own, he realized it had not been his imagination. There was something utterly enchanting in her sweet innocence. Something that made him tremble with the mad desire to drown in that sweetness. To stir to life the ready passion he could sense just below the surface.

And yet, even as he felt her tentative response, she was pulling away from him and fleeing to the sanctuary of her chambers.

His first instinct had been to pursue her and force her to admit that she did still desire him. His aching body practically demanded that he put an end to the unnatural lack of physical relations between them.

But he had forced himself to deny the fierce impulse. He had to be patient, he told himself. He did not want to push Beatrice into a relationship she was not yet prepared to accept. When he did make her his wife, he wanted her eager and thoroughly prepared for the moment.

All very noble, he thought with a stab of self-mockery. Unfortunately his good intentions had accomplished nothing more than allowing Beatrice to retreat even further behind her prickly defenses. He had not so much as caught a glimpse of her the rest of the day, and even this evening she had sent down a polite message claiming she did not feel well enough to join them for dinner.

Clearly she deeply regretted her momentary lapse and had retreated to reinforce her icy composure.

Gabriel swallowed another mouthful of the port, wanting nothing more than to charge upstairs and pummel down her door. It was that or drink himself into a stupor, he acknowledged wryly.

Perhaps sensing Gabriel's brooding annoyance, the silent vicar seated across the table gently cleared his throat.

"It is unfortunate that Beatrice was not feeling well enough to come down to dinner," he said in cautious tones. "I hope it is nothing serious. She seemed to be quite well earlier today."

Gabriel could not prevent his wry smile. "Oh, I doubt that it is anything life-threatening."

As if disturbed by Gabriel's overt lack of sympathy for his ailing wife, Humbly offered a slight frown. "Have you called for a doctor?"

Gabriel shrugged. "There is no need."

"Are you certain?"

"Quite certain." Gabriel set his glass on the table with a distinct bang. "I am the reason Beatrice refused to come down to dinner."

"Oh." Humbly paused to digest the abrupt confession, then, hesitantly, he leaned forward. "Forgive me for being an interfering busybody, but was there an argument?"

Gabriel instinctively stiffened at the bold intrusion into a very private matter between a husband and wife. But the genuine sympathy that glittered in the sherry eyes eased his initial irritation.

The old gentleman truly seemed to care about Beatrice. Perhaps he could be the one to talk some sense into her.

"On the contrary," he forced himself to admit slowly. "We actually managed to share a pleasant conversation. And then . . ."

"Yes?" the vicar prompted.

"Beatrice momentarily forgot to hate me."

"But that is wonderful."

"So I thought at the time." His fingers tightened on the glass until the delicate crystal threatened to shatter. "Unfortunately she has obviously had second thoughts and now regrets her brief lapse. I have no doubt she is in her room, grimly restoring her walls of forbidding ice."

Humbly heaved a faint sigh. "It is not easy for Beatrice."

Gabriel frowned in exasperation. "I realize that, Humbly. But she is making this far more difficult than it has to be. We could do better."

"Yes, indeed," Humbly was swift to agree. "Beatrice must be made to see that she is only hurting herself."

"I do not suppose you have a brilliant notion as to how I could accomplish that amazing feat?" he inquired in dry tones.

There was a moment's pause before Humbly gave an offhand shrug. "You should woo her."

"What?"

The older man smiled at Gabriel's sharp confusion. "Beatrice feels as if she has been tricked into this marriage. You must now give her a desire to be your wife."

Lucifer's teeth. Did the vicar believe he had not tried for weeks to convince Beatrice that he could bring her happiness if only she would allow him to?

"What would you have me do?" he demanded in a disgruntled voice. "Buy her gifts with her own money?"

Humbly gave a chastising click of his tongue. "Certainly not. Beatrice has no interest in lavish gifts."

"Then what?"

"What does she prefer?"

Gabriel considered a moment before giving a shrug. "Those damnable machines."

"Yes."

Gabriel regarded the vicar with a measure of suspicion. "You do not propose that I try my hand at inventions? I should no doubt burn the house down or explode us all to the netherworld."

Humbly gave a soft chuckle. "I was thinking more in terms of helping in her hobby."

"I know nothing of such things."

"Surely there is some means to be of service?" Humbly persisted.

"How?" Gabriel threw himself back in his seat with a display of impatience. "I warned you that I was hopeless at such things."

"You managed well enough before you were wed. Beatrice did, after all, choose you as her husband over any of her other suitors."

Gabriel gave a short, humorless laugh. "Much to her disgust."

"Her pride and heart are wounded at the moment. You must restore her faith in you. And more important, in herself."

His odd choice of words caught Gabriel off guard. He narrowed his gaze as he regarded the round countenance.

"In herself?"

Humbly appeared startled by his seeming stupidity.

"Surely you realize that Beatrice has never possessed much belief in her own worth beyond her fortune?"

Gabriel was instantly offended by the condemning description of his bride.

"Ridiculous," he retorted in dangerous tones. Not even this harmless vicar would be allowed to insult Beatrice. Not within his hearing. "She is an extraordinarily intelligent woman with an endless number of talents. Beyond that she is kind and loyal and utterly without artifice."

Perhaps unable to sense he was very close to having his cork drawn, Humbly stabbed Gabriel with a stern gaze.

"However, she has never possessed the conventional attractions desired in a maiden. Unlike most young women, she has never been a beauty or especially charming. And not even I can claim she is anything but a wretched musician. Instead, she possesses a fascinating mind and the heart of an inventor. Is it any wonder she has been taught to doubt her desirability for a gentleman?"

Gabriel opened his mouth to deny the ridiculous words only to hesitate as he realized there was more than a bit of truth to the vicar's description of Beatrice.

He had witnessed for himself the numerous members of the *ton* who had laughed behind Beatrice's back at her eccentric notions and unpolished manners. Certainly no more than a handful of notorious fortune hunters ever sought her company.

A sharp, nearly unbearable ache filled his heart.

How alone she must have felt among the glittering society. As alone as he had felt after his mother's death.

His features twisted with a rueful regret. "And I only ensured her belief that she is unworthy," he said roughly.

Humbly smiled sadly. "I fear so."

"Bloody hell." Gabriel banged his hand on the table with enough force to make the vicar nearly tumble from his chair in surprise. "Forgive me, Humbly. What a tangle this all is. I truly did not mean to bring her harm."

"I believe you, my son," the older man said gently.

"But will Beatrice?"

"That is in your hands."

"So you say." Gabriel grimaced, thinking of his wife's icy composure. It was a wonder he did not go about with a permanent case of frostbite. "I would rather face an entire French regiment than my own wife. They were much less terrifying."

"It is not Beatrice that terrifies you," Humbly corrected Gabriel in firm tones.

For a moment Gabriel thought he must have misunderstood the vicar. "What?"

He gave a lift of his plump hands. "I fear it is your own

sense of guilt that troubles you. When you look upon Beatrice, you worry you have sacrificed her happiness to save your estate."

Gabriel's hands clenched at the accusation. He did not have the luxury of possessing a guilty conscience. His heavy duty ensured that.

"I did what I had to do," he said harshly.

"What you believed you must do," Humbly corrected him.

Gabriel gritted his teeth. "Yes."

"And you have no regrets?"

"Of course I do," he rasped, feeling unbearably harassed. What did this man want from him? "As I said, I never wished to hurt Beatrice. When I wed her, it was with every intention of being a kind and devoted husband."

"And there was no guilt for having deceived her in the first place?"

Gabriel slowly narrowed his gaze. He sensed the vicar was attempting to force him to examine the complex emotions he had determinedly kept hidden deep in his heart. Emotions he was uncertain that he wanted examined.

"I believe you are a rather dangerous opponent, Vicar."

Humbly gave a flustered wave of his hands. "No, no. Merely an old and rather foolish man."

Gabriel smiled with wry amusement, not deceived for a moment.

"You are correct, of course," he admitted reluctantly. "I did sacrifice Beatrice for my own selfish purposes. And I did so in a cold-blooded, methodical manner. Like the villain she has named me, I chose her deliberately because she was vulnerable and appeared to possess the qualities necessary for my countess, most important her very large dowry."

Humbly raised his shaggy brows. "You found nothing to attract you to her beyond her money?"

Gabriel gave a restless shrug, not wishing to discuss the odd sense of awareness he had experienced when he had first been introduced to Beatrice. The vicar would think he was daft if he revealed that he had felt as if he and Beatrice were destined to be together by some mystical fate.

"I admire her intelligence, of course," he said in carefully controlled tones. "And she has proven to be very good with the tenants and villagers. I cannot walk out the door without being told of her generosity and concern for the people of Falcon Park." An unwittingly fond smile curved his lips. "You claim that she possesses no charm, but she has won the hearts and loyalty of the neighborhood with astonishing swiftness."

"This pleases you?" Humbly demanded.

"Of course." Gabriel regarded his guest with a faint frown. "It is very important that the Countess of Faulconer be respected by those who are vital to the future of our estate."

"So, you have a beginning," Humbly announced with a complacent smile. "You have Falcon Park between you."

Gabriel was unimpressed with the man's logic. "She is not likely to offer more."

"Not without a measure of proper wooing."

An exasperated sigh was wrenched from Gabriel's throat. "We are back to that, eh? Gads, I feel like a raw recruit again, bumbling about with no notion of how to go on."

The round countenance abruptly hardened. "You thought of your needs when you wed Beatrice. Now it is time to consider her needs. I believe you to be a good man, my lord. Look into your heart and you will find a means of reaching your wife."

Gabriel silently considered the chastising words.

Could it be possible?

Could Beatrice's distant heart be won?

He drew in a deep, fortifying breath. He had hoped time would heal Beatrice's wounds. That eventually, with enough patience, she would be able to put the past behind her and she would come to accept her role as his wife.

But perhaps Humbly was correct. It could be that beneath Beatrice's practical nature was the heart of a romantic. Maybe she desired to be swept off her feet rather than being left to brood upon her ill treatment.

One thing was for certain, he wryly conceded, he could not make more of a hash of his marriage than he already had.

Rising early, Gabriel made his daily tour of his lands and spoke with his tenants before returning to the house and making his way to the busy kitchen. Less than a quarter of an hour later he had a large tray that he carefully carried toward Beatrice's chambers.

He hesitated more than once as he made his way through the vast corridors. He was far from certain that he was not making a complete ass of himself. Beatrice had never indicated a desire to be wooed by her husband. Indeed, she had been wretchedly clear that she wished to be left in peace.

Still, he continued his march to her distant chambers.

He had to at least know that he had tried his best to make Beatrice happy. She deserved that much.

And besides, what was the worst that could happen?

A plate of eggs dumped upon his head?

A blackened eye?

He had survived worse indignities before.

Almost reassured, Gabriel halted in front of the door to Beatrice's rooms and with as much luck as skill managed to push it open without spilling the tray onto the floor.

Relieved to have passed the first barrier, Gabriel angled his way toward the vast canopy bed that dominated the room.

He perched on the edge of the mattress, watching his wife as she stirred beneath the covers.

A smile curved his lips at her flushed features and tumble of honey curls. She looked softly feminine in her sleep. Almost vulnerable without the driving energy that crackled about her when she was awake.

The urge to lean down and kiss the satin softness of her lips was halted as her thick lashes fluttered upward and the amber eyes regarded him in a dazed fashion.

"Good morning, my dear," he said softly.

With awkward motions she struggled to a seated position, careful to keep the covers tucked to her chin.

"Gabriel, what are you doing?"

"Since you are not feeling well, I thought I would bring you your breakfast in bed."

With a flourish he placed the tray across her knees. Glancing at the numerous plates, she possessed the grace to blush.

"Oh. I—I am much improved this morning."

"I am happy to hear that, but there is no reason to waste a perfectly good breakfast. I have brought your favorites. Fresh strawberries, eggs, a bit of ham, and plenty of buttered toast."

Obviously flustered and caught off guard by his unexpected appearance, she struggled to hide her unease.

"Thank you."

"Here." Scooting until his hip pressed intimately against the curve of her thigh, Gabriel reached out to pluck the napkin from the tray and carefully tucked it beneath her chin.

Her tongue peeked out to dampen her lips. Gabriel caught his breath as sweet heat spread through him.

"Are you not needed in the fields?" she demanded warily.

"I have already been to ensure the hay is being properly turned and the dykes cleared. I believe they are capable of surviving a few hours without me." He smiled gently. "Are you not going to eat?"

"Of course." With jerky motions she reached for a strawberry and stuffed it into her mouth. Gabriel hid a smile. At least she had not tossed the tray at his head or toppled him off the bed.

It was a start.

"I presume that you managed to halt Chalfrey from creating a mutiny in our garden?"

"Barely." She absently toyed with a slice of toast. "He is quite adamant that the least amount of change is near sacrilege."

Gabriel regarded her steadily. "He could easily be replaced."

As expected, Beatrice shook her head firmly. For all her brisk competency, she possessed a surprisingly tender heart.

At least for all but him, he acknowledged wryly.

"No. For all his grumbling, I believe he is a good gardener, and no one could possibly devote themselves to Falcon Park more fiercely than he does."

"True enough." He gave an approving nod. "And I do not doubt that he will soon be as loyal to you as he was to my mother." He paused as he studied her bluntly carved features. "You remind me a great deal of her, you know."

"Your mother?" She gave a sudden frown. "Impossible."

He lifted his brows at her adamant tone. "Why?"

"I have seen her portrait. She was very lovely and very elegant. Not at all like me."

He smiled wryly at her stiff tone. Had her parents never forced her to realize the beauty of those amazing amber eyes? Or the temptation of her lush curves?

"You are lovely as well, Beatrice," he insisted. "But I was speaking more of her concern for the staff and tenants. Unlike my father, she devoted herself to improving the lives of those who depended upon my family. I still recall how the children in the village would gather about her the moment she stepped down from the carriage. They quite simply adored her. It made me very proud that she was my mother."

Although Beatrice made a valiant effort, she could not entirely hide her pleasure at his words.

"I should have liked to have met her," she at last murmured.

Gabriel felt the familiar pang of loss at the thought of his mother. He too wished she were alive to meet Beatrice. He did not doubt for a moment that the two would have gotten along famously.

"You would have loved her." He slowly smiled. "And she would have considered you a very fine countess."

A faint hint of color bloomed beneath her fair skin. "How old were you when she died?"

"Nine." He thought back to that horrible time. "It was quite unexpected. She had gone to help a tenant, when she was caught in a sudden storm. Two days later she was dead."

The amber eyes softened with sympathy. "That must have been very difficult for you."

"It took me a long time to realize she was never coming back." His lips twisted. "I would creep into this room in the middle of the night and sleep in her bed just in case she suddenly came home. I wanted to be the first to greet her. At last my father began locking the door so I could not enter."

An odd expression rippled over her countenance. "This is her room?"

"Of course. And the door still stays locked. Rather ironic, is it not?"

He instantly regretted the unthinking words as Beatrice stiffened.

"Gabriel."

"No, forgive me, Beatrice." He reached out to gently brush a honey curl from her cheek. "I was only teasing you."

For a moment he thought he had ruined what measure of progress he had made, then much to his relief, her tension eased.

"Does it bother you that I have had the chambers refurbished?"

"Gads, no." He glanced about the cheerful room that was so very different from the gloomy squalor that had dominated it for far too long. "I loved my mother, not these chambers. Besides, even as a child I found this room drafty and the furnishings shabby. Now it is a room fit for a countess. My countess."

Their gazes tangled and Gabriel was suddenly aware that they were very much alone and very conveniently situated upon a comfortable bed.

He wanted to lean forward and claim those lips that haunted his dreams. He wanted to cover her body with his own and lose himself in the passion he knew smoldered within her. He wanted to hear her cry out in pleasure as he made her his own.

His body stirred to aching life, but as if sensing the

quicksilver heat in the air, Beatrice shifted uneasily upon the pillows.

"I should be rising. I have an appointment soon," she abruptly announced.

Gabriel reluctantly reined in his straining desire.

At least Beatrice was speaking to him again, he attempted to ease his frustration. And they had managed a conversation that did not include the usual bickering and bitter accusations.

It was progress, even if his body did protest at being denied the full pleasure of possessing a wife.

Perhaps this business of wooing his bride was not so noddy after all.

"Of course." Rising to his feet, he offered her a gentle smile. "I shall see you later."

Six

Beatrice had a dozen tasks awaiting her attention.

There were pattern books to be examined.

An artist demanding her opinion on the painting he was restoring.

The cook requesting she review the day's menu.

Several letters that remained upon her desk.

And the household accounts that she had not so much as glanced through.

But while a corner of her mind chastised her for falling behind on her duties, the larger part of her thoughts were in a rare muddle.

It was absurd.

For weeks she had managed to live at Falcon Park without being disturbed by Gabriel. Oh, certainly there were the occasional spats that ended in sharp words. And she could not in all honesty deny that her dreams were far too often consumed with thoughts of her husband.

But with sheer willpower she had managed to establish an existence as Lady Faulconer that was as comfortable as she could hope for under the circumstances.

She had her duty to the tenants, the all-consuming passion for restoring Falcon Park, and her inventions. It was not the life she had envisioned. It was, however, preferable to the sudden unpredictability of the past few days.

Pacing across the small room she had claimed as her study, Beatrice attempted to soothe her tangled nerves.

Perhaps she was merely overreacting, she told herself. After all, what had actually occurred to make her so uneasy?

Granted, Gabriel was behaving in a peculiar fashion. He had begun to seek her out with unnerving regularity. He readily discussed his most intimate emotions. And there was a new determination in his countenance that she did not entirely trust. But he had not precisely forced his attentions upon her.

Instead, he had been utterly charming and startlingly vulnerable.

And that was precisely the problem, she reluctantly conceded.

Since arriving in Derbyshire, Gabriel had rarely attempted to push past her icy wall of disdain. Rather, he had allowed her to establish a sense of independence. Only on rare occasions had his patience snapped and he had revealed the frustration that simmered at their strained relationship.

This sudden return to the persistent, tantalizing gentleman who had stolen her heart was, to say the least, disconcerting.

How was she to remain indifferent to him when he shared the loneliness of his childhood? Or his deep regret he had somehow failed those who depended upon him? Or when he pulled her in his arms and kissed her as if he truly desired her?

Remembering the sharp, poignant awareness that had rushed through her as Gabriel had sat upon her bed that morning, Beatrice pressed a hand to her erratic heart.

Yesterday she had fled from his kiss with every intention of ensuring she never reveal such weakness again.

But while she had devoted a goodly portion of the night to sternly lecturing herself, she had been no more prepared for Gabriel's appearance in her bedchamber than if she had never bothered.

And that, of course, was what was forcing her to pace the floor rather than concentrating upon her waiting duties.

Telling herself that she was being all sorts of a fool, Beatrice turned about to force her reluctant feet to carry her to her desk. She would not waste her entire day.

Unfortunately, she had just made her decision, when the object of her turmoil abruptly strolled through the open door.

Beatrice froze, her gaze drinking in the sight of his lean frame exquisitely revealed by the tailored blue coat and buff breeches. The plain, almost severe style suited his innate elegance that had no need for wadding or corsets. He was far too handsome and compelling for the fripperies of dandies.

It was little wonder she always felt a frump in his presence, she ruefully acknowledged, painfully aware that her gown was already streaked with dust and her hair escaping from the knot atop her head.

If Gabriel found her appearance less than flattering, however, he was careful to keep his distaste well hidden as he moved to stand before her with a potent smile.

"Beatrice, may I have a moment?" he murmured.

Ignoring the rather giddy pleasure that raced through her at his unexpected appearance, Beatrice summoned a composed expression.

"There is not another battle in the gardens, I trust?"

He chuckled. "Not to my knowledge."

"What is it?"

"I have something I wish you to see."

She regarded him with a hint of wariness. What the devil was he up to now?

"Very well," she slowly agreed.

Allowing him to take her hand and place it upon his arm, they left the study and headed down the stairs. She could not deny a burning curiosity at what he could possibly wish her to see.

They had just reached the foyer when they were halted by a large woman with gray hair and a harried expression.

"Oh, Lady Faulconer," the housekeeper cried in relief.

Coming to a halt, Beatrice regarded the servant with a lift of her brows.

"Yes, Mrs. Greene?"

"Vicar Dunder sent a message that Mrs. Litton has fallen and taken to her bed. He wished you to ensure that she has a proper dinner."

On the point of assuring Mrs. Greene that she would see to the elderly widow, Beatrice was halted as Gabriel abruptly stepped forward.

"You may tell the vicar that a basket of food will be delivered to Mrs. Litton and that for today he can attend to his duties rather than devoting his attention to the ale at the local inn. You will also tell him that Lord Faulconer is far from satisfied with his efforts among his flock. Perhaps he will be so good as to meet with me so we can discuss the precise nature of his responsibilities."

Beatrice gasped at the less than subtle threat, but oddly, Mrs. Greene appeared rather pleased at the message she was commanded to deliver.

"Very good, my lord."

The woman returned down the hall, and Beatrice found herself being led out of the house and toward the distant stables.

"Was that necessary?" she at last demanded, not at all certain what to expect next from her husband.

The features that had been darkened by the sun tightened with displeasure.

"I am weary of the fool passing his burdens on to you, my dear."

She glanced at him in surprise. "I enjoy helping the tenants."

"Yes, but you are very busy with the workmen, as well as your inventors. You should schedule your visits with the tenants upon your pleasure, not the vicar's. You are not his servant. I will not have you exhausted."

Caught off guard as much by the sharp concern in his tone as by the realization he was far more aware of her busy schedule than she had suspected, Beatrice could only give a slow nod of her head.

"As you wish."

Suddenly spotting a footman headed to the house with a large basket of flowers from the hothouses, Gabriel beckoned him forward. Then, with seeming concentration, he sorted through the various blooms.

"Let me see. Not a rose," he murmured, at last plucking out a daisy and waving the footman on his way. "You, my dear, are a daisy. Unassuming, with a delicate fragrance that does not seek to overpower, but instead provides a subtle sweetness."

Pressing the daisy into her hand, Gabriel once again tugged her toward the outbuildings. Beatrice was barely aware of where they were headed as she regarded him with growing suspicion.

"What is it, Gabriel?" she at last blurted out.

He slanted her a puzzled glance. "What do you mean?"

"You have been behaving very oddly."

"Have I?"

"Yes."

He shrugged, a mysterious smile tugging his full lips. "I am merely determined to enjoy a few days' rest after a difficult planting season. That is surely not so surprising?"

"I suppose not," she reluctantly conceded, although she did not believe for a moment that his peculiar behavior had anything to do with the end of the planting season.

No doubt sensing her inner distrust, Gabriel abruptly angled away from the stables and pulled her toward a large barn.

"This way."

"Where are we going?" she demanded.

"You will see." Surprisingly, he did not turn from the barn but instead led her through the open door and toward the center of the long, empty structure. "What do you think?"

Beatrice glanced around the musty building with a frown. "I think it is a barn."

"Yes, it is in need of work, but it is well built and it possesses ample room."

She gave a lift of her hands. "It is a fine barn."

The hazel eyes shimmered in the dim light. "I thought it could be a suitable location for you to view your inventions."

Stunned, Beatrice felt her mouth drop open. "Oh."

"I will have a fireplace built and I thought you would wish for a desk and a few chairs. It will not be perfect, but at least you will not have to stand in the rain, and it will be considerably warmer when winter arrives."

Beatrice abruptly turned away, knowing she could not hide her reaction to his kind gesture. No one had ever encouraged her unfashionable interest in inventions. Indeed, she had been continually browbeaten by her family into discovering a more conventional pastime.

The very knowledge that Gabriel was willing to support her in such a tangible manner sent a dangerous flood of warmth through her heart.

"Yes," she at last whispered.

"Do you think it will do?"

She was forced to clear her throat. "I think that it will do very well."

"Then I shall have a few of the workmen begin on it immediately."

Beatrice slowly turned back to face her husband. "Gabriel."

"Yes?"

"Thank you."

He moved slowly forward to grasp her hands, careful not to crush the delicate daisy.

"I only wish you to be happy here, Beatrice. It is what I have always wanted."

She nodded. This man had ruthlessly sought her out to gain control of her fortune. He had deliberately won her affections while hiding his own devious purpose. She had sworn she would never forgive his treachery.

But gazing into those hazel eyes, Beatrice found herself wondering if he did care in some small way.

"It is not easy," she said in uneven tones.

Gabriel smiled ruefully. "No. I realize that it will take time."

He stepped closer, almost as if he intended to kiss her. Beatrice felt her breath quicken with anticipation. She did not even think of turning away. Not when she trembled with the force of her need. She wanted to feel his lips upon her own. To taste that magical desire that only Gabriel could inspire.

But even as his gaze lowered to her slightly parted lips,

there was a sudden echo of scurrying footsteps, and then the rotund form of Mr. Humbly darted through the doorway.

For a moment the older man merely stood in the shadows, as if attempting to catch his breath. It was only after his eyes adjusted to the gloom that he noticed Beatrice and Gabriel regarding him with startled gazes.

"Oh . . . forgive me," he muttered, a rather flustered heat staining his round countenance.

"Mr. Humbly." Beatrice stepped forward. "Is anything amiss?"

"No, no. Just enjoying a bit of fresh air."

His smile held a sweet innocence, but his subterfuge was swiftly foiled as the shrill voice of Aunt Sarah drifted through the air.

"Mr. Humbly."

Beatrice conjured a teasingly shocked expression. "Why, Mr. Humbly, are you deliberately avoiding Aunt Sarah?"

"Ah . . . " The vicar straightened the hat that was about to tumble from his head and gave an uncomfortable cough. "Well . . ."

Gabriel gave a sympathetic chuckle. "Do not fear, Humbly. We shall not reveal your whereabouts."

The vicar gave a small bow. "I am in your debt, my lord."

"I must meet with my steward. If you will excuse me?" Gabriel turned to lift Beatrice's hand and lightly kissed her fingers. He smiled deeply into her startled eyes before nodding toward Humbly and walking from the barn.

Beatrice watched his retreat with a puzzled frown, the daisy still clutched in her hand.

She did not trust Gabriel in this odd mood, she told herself. His capricious manner left her stomach tangled in knots and her thoughts in turmoil. No, it was not precisely Gabriel that she did not trust. It was her own reaction to his sudden overtures of friendship.

It had been a simple matter to hold on to her hurt at his betrayal when she encountered him only on a rare occasion. It was quite another when he was showering her with attention.

"Beatrice."

Suddenly realizing Mr. Humbly was speaking to her, Beatrice made an effort to concentrate upon the kindly vicar.

"Forgive me, I was woolgathering," she admitted. "What did you say?"

"I inquired if you were troubled."

She smiled rather wryly. "Why do you ask?"

"You have a very odd expression upon your countenance."

"No. Nothing is troubling me. It is just . . ."

"What?" the older gentleman prompted as he moved forward to closely scrutinize her shadowed countenance.

Beatrice gave a restless shrug. "Lord Faulconer has suggested that I use this barn to view the inventions that are brought for my inspection."

"But that is a wonderful notion," Humbly retorted in satisfaction. "So much more comfortable than standing in the wind."

"Yes," she agreed dubiously.

"Then why are you frowning?"

"It is odd."

"What is?"

"I have never had anyone but you understand my interest in inventions." She confessed her inner disturbance. "As you know, my parents were very disapproving of such an interest. Not only because young ladies should concentrate upon delicate tasks such as painting and embroidery, but because they claimed that they needed no reminders that their vast wealth came from my grandfather's patents. Even my few friends think it far too vulgar to be readily discussed."

Humbly gave a wise nod of his head. "Few among society consider it fashionable to possess original thoughts or interests. Like sheep, they strive to huddle together and follow their leader with blind devotion. I am thankful that Lord Faulconer possesses the sense to admire your unique qualities."

Beatrice absently gnawed her full bottom lip. "Or else he is merely humoring me."

Without warning Humbly gave a tinkling laugh. "He is now your husband. By law he is your master. There is no need to humor you," he said with unshakable logic. "He obviously is attempting to encourage what pleases you the most. A very admirable sentiment."

Beatrice regarded the vicar with a growing suspicion. It occurred to her that Gabriel's peculiar behavior began only after the arrival of Mr. Humbly. And certainly she would not put it past the older gentleman to interfere in her marriage. He always did possess a habit of dabbling in the lives of others.

"Did you ask him to do this?" she demanded bluntly.

Humbly appeared suitably shocked by the accusation. "Not at all. I will admit that Lord Faulconer confessed he was saddened by your obvious unhappiness, but I could offer him no reassurances beyond patience."

Beatrice was not wholly convinced. Humbly could be as cunning as a fox when he chose.

"I will not be charmed into forgetting how I was duped," she said in uneven tones.

Humbly reached out to pat her hand. "Of course not."

"I was fooled once before. I could not bear to be fooled again."

"I do not believe that Lord Faulconer seeks to fool you, Beatrice."

How easy it was for him to be so certain, she acknowledged with a grimace. She had trusted her instincts before, only to discover they were flawed. She would not be so swift to depend upon them again.

"I must return to the house. If you will excuse me."

With a distracted expression Beatrice turned to make her way from the barn. She could devote the entire day to brooding upon Gabriel's sudden displays of kindness. She knew, however, there were no answers to be found in her chaotic thoughts.

Thankfully she had more than enough work demanding her attention.

Moving across the stable yard, Beatrice paid scant attention to her surroundings. She instead considered whether to meet with the workmen or pacify her anxious cook that the meal chosen for that evening was acceptable.

Such dilemmas were far simpler to solve than the mysteries of the heart.

Her steps slowed and too late she suddenly noted the fretful woman hurrying in her direction.

Blast.

Why had she not recalled that Aunt Sarah was lurking the grounds in search of her victim?

It was too late now to dodge into the stables, and Beatrice reluctantly halted as the widow eagerly hurried to her side.

"Oh, Beatrice, I am glad I have found you. I have been searching for dear Mr. Humbly."

Beatrice smiled in a vague manner. "Have you?"

"Yes, such a lovely gentleman." Aunt Sarah heaved a romantic sigh.

"He is indeed."

"And he possesses his own cottage."

"Yes."

A decidedly speculative gleam entered the older woman's eyes. "And I suppose he has a comfortable income?"

Beatrice thought of poor Mr. Humbly still hiding in the barn. Although there was a decided humor in watching the gentleman desperately attempt to avoid the clutches of Aunt Sarah, she could not in all conscience allow it to continue. He was really far too sweet to be badgered in such a manner.

"I shouldn't think he has much of an income at all." She determinedly dashed the hopes of the older woman. "His family has always been in straitened circumstances, and a vicar is rarely given more than a pittance for his services."

Aunt Sarah was not so easily discouraged. "Yes, but a vicar living simply must have some savings?"

Beatrice shook her head. "Not Mr. Humbly. He has far too often taken from his own pocket when he encounters another in need. His own comfort has never been his concern."

"I see," Aunt Sarah murmured, a frown beginning to form on her brow. Clearly she was not overly eager to wed a vicar who could offer nothing more than a damp cottage and few amenities.

"Do not fear. As you said, Mr. Humbly prefers to live simply. He will no doubt be satisfied in his small cottage with the barest of necessities."

"I suppose," Aunt Sarah agreed reluctantly, then without warning her countenance abruptly cleared. "Unless . . . "

Beatrice did not like the sly glint in the older woman's eye.

"Yes?"

Aunt Sarah smiled with satisfaction. "Why, obviously those who care for him will do what is necessary to ensure he is well cared for in his later years. Surely it is the duty of his friends to provide an adequate income?"

Beatrice had to admire the woman's cunning. She had clearly determined that Beatrice would do whatever possible to please Mr. Humbly. Including offering a portion of her fortune to keep him and his wife in luxury.

"I do not believe Mr. Humbly would accept charity," she said sternly.

"Charity? La." Aunt Sarah easily dismissed the notion. She possessed no scruples, expecting others to provide for her welfare. "'Tis no less than he deserves."

"Perhaps," Beatrice admitted ruefully, realizing she had been outgunned. Poor Humbly would have to face this battle on his own. "If you will excuse me, I have a great many duties to attend to."

Beatrice continued her path to the house, on this occasion keeping her pace brisk enough to avoid any further interruptions.

She made a brief halt in the kitchens to speak with Cook before seeking out the workmen and at last the artist who refused to touch the seventeenth-century canvas without being allowed to travel to London with it and have it examined by the Royal Academy of Art.

All in all, it was nearly four hours before she could make her way to her chambers. She felt in dire need of a hot bath and rest before returning downstairs for dinner.

Pushing open the door to her chamber, she stepped inside. She had taken only a few steps before she came to an abrupt halt.

"Good heavens," she breathed, her startled gaze moving over the vast bouquets of daisies that were banked about the room.

Standing beside the bed, Beatrice's maid flashed her a wide grin. "They are a real treat, are they not, ma'am?"

Beatrice was stunned. "Where did they come from?"

"Lord Faulconer had them sent from every hothouse in the neighborhood," the servant confessed in pleased tones. "There is also a note."

Walking toward the dresser where the maid was pointing, Beatrice retrieved the brief message written in Gabriel's bold hand.

> *Beatrice,*
>   *I hope these flowers bring you pleasure and perhaps a smile to your lips. I wish you only happiness.*
>   *Yours to command,*
>   *Gabriel*

Beatrice dropped the note and pressed a hand to her heart.

Dear heavens.

How was she possibly to resist such charming advances?

And more important, did she truly want to resist?

Gads, what a devilish coil.

Seven

The cottage was small but ruthlessly clean, with new thatching and a handful of well-made furnishings. There was also the sweet smell of fresh flowers that Beatrice had brought along with a large basket of food.

Already having coaxed a bowl of warm soup into Mrs. Litton's hands along with a slice of freshly baked bread, Beatrice settled in a chair close to the bed and watched the widow enjoy the small feast.

She had not lied to Gabriel. She did enjoy her moments spent in the company of the tenants. Unlike the more sophisticated *ton*, the people of Falcon Park were honest and straightforward. They did not twitter behind their fans or smile sweetly as poison dripped from their lips. They did not judge others by the beauty of their countenance or elegance of their manners.

Instead, they worked hard and expected the same of others. They also offered a genuine friendship that was based upon loyalty and respect.

It was little wonder she felt far more comfortable in the company of common farmers than in the presence of aristocrats.

Scooping up the last of the hearty soup, the older woman leaned back with a sigh.

"Delicious," she murmured, her alert gaze at odds with her frail body covered by a woolen blanket. Mrs. Litton might be well into her seventies, but her wits were as sharp as ever and her tongue embarrassingly blunt. "So kind of you, my lady."

"Not at all." Beatrice set the empty tray aside and smiled at the widow. "It is a pleasure to have an excuse to visit you."

A rather mysterious expression settled upon the lined face as Mrs. Litton regarded her.

"So much like the last countess," she said in satisfaction. "She could always make a soul feel comfortable about her no matter what their station in life. I am pleased the Falcon blessing was not lost with the death of the eldest son."

Beatrice gave a startled blink. "Blessing?"

Mrs. Litton tilted her head to one side, suddenly looking for all the world like a curious bird.

"Surely you have heard the story of the first Lord Faulconer, who saved a wounded falcon from certain death?"

"No."

"Ah." The pale eyes glittered with amusement at Beatrice's baffled expression. "The falcon was a magical creature, you see, and after being rescued it gave Lord Faulconer the blessing of a true-hearted mate. Since that day, all the Lord Faulconers have wed women of courage and loyalty. Women such as yourself."

Beatrice felt her face flood with color. Dear heavens, was it not bad enough to be thrust into the position of countess? Must she also live up to the absurd notion of some ancient legend?

It was enough to make any sensible woman flee in terror.

Realizing that Mrs. Litton was awaiting her response, Beatrice forced herself to smile in a calm manner.

"It is a lovely story."

"Aye." The widow paused for a moment. "A pity not all the Lord Faulconers have been equally loyal and courageous. I'm not one to speak ill of the dead, but the previous earl was a proper rapscallion. Not many could mourn his passing."

Beatrice was well enough acquainted with the older woman not to be shocked by her unflattering words. She had made little secret of her disgust for the previous Lord Faulconer.

"I am certain it must have been a difficult time for the tenants," Beatrice sympathized.

The older woman gave a snort. "A sorry time it was. Many a good man was forced to poaching or even thievery to keep his family fed. Pride don't put food on the table."

Beatrice gave a slow nod of understanding. Desperation would drive even the most worthy man to behavior foreign to his nature.

Such as forcing an honorable gentleman to deceive a young maiden, a treacherous voice whispered in the back of her mind.

She swiftly crushed the renegade thought.

That was entirely different, she assured herself.

Entirely different.

"I can assure you that things will be much better from now on," she forced herself to say in even tones.

"Aye. The new earl is a rare treat." Mrs. Litton gave a low chuckle. "Of course, at first the tenants were not sure of him. He left Falcon Park quickly enough when he were young, and there were those who thought he would bleed the estate dry just as his father. You could have knocked the men down with a feather when instead he showed up in the fields day after day, as if he were one of them."

Beatrice did not doubt that Gabriel had been something of a shock after his father's selfish indifference.

"Lord Faulconer is very eager to ensure the welfare of the estate as well as those who depend upon him."

"A good man. I cannot say what a difference he has made already. He has given us hope, which is a good sight more than we've had in many a year."

"Yes."

A speculative gleam entered the pale eyes. "And handsome in the bargain. All that remains is to begin filling that nursery with heirs."

Beatrice surged awkwardly to her feet. Good Lord. It had not occurred to her until that moment that the entire estate would be carefully watching for signs that she was breeding.

Producing an heir, after all, was the single most important duty for a countess. More important than charitable works or managing her household. Certainly more important than discovering a new invention.

It was unnerving to realize that her most intimate life would be openly speculated on by so many. Unnerving and more than a little embarrassing.

"I must go," she muttered, knowing her cheeks were rosy. "You will let me know if there is anything you need?"

"My daughter will be here tomorrow. There's no need to be fretting about me any longer."

"I enjoy my visits, as you well know," Beatrice assured the older woman. "I shall return in a day or two."

Leaving the used dishes to be collected by a servant, Beatrice made her way through the cramped cottage and slipped through the door. Although she dearly cared for Mrs. Litton, she could not deny it was a relief to be away from that searching gaze. The old woman was far too crafty not to realize she had struck a raw nerve.

Combined with the knowledge that Gabriel and Beatrice lived coldly separate lives, it would take little imagination to realize that there would be no heir.

At least not in the foreseeable future.

Angling toward the path that would lead back toward the main house, Beatrice's gaze narrowed as she caught sight of a lone daisy lying upon the dirt. She bent down to scoop up the flower, wondering where it had come from. It was rather a peculiar place to find a daisy. Then she shrugged. No doubt it had blown from the hothouse or dropped from some hopeful swain's hand.

She continued onward, only to come to a halt as she discovered yet another daisy lying directly in the path.

"What the devil?" With a frown she hurried forward, finding yet another daisy just around the bend.

It was obvious now that someone had deliberately placed the flowers upon the path.

But why?

Intrigued, Beatrice hurried down the path, following the trail of daisies even when they led her past the house and down toward the lake. She had nearly reached the edge of the water, when she turned her head to discover the familiar gentleman leaning negligently against a small rowboat that was pulled onto the shore.

"Gabriel," she breathed, not truly surprised to discover her husband responsible for the daisies. Who else had ever compared her to the lovely flower?

With a smile he shoved himself upright. In the golden sunlight he appeared vibrantly male and breathtakingly handsome. She shivered as the coiled energy that seemed to surround him reached out to send a rash of awareness over her skin.

"I hoped that the daises would lead you to me," he murmured.

Beatrice attempted to ignore the charm that lay thick in the air.

"What is this about?"

"It is such a lovely day, I hoped that I could lure you out for a picnic upon the island."

Beatrice glanced toward the small island in the middle of the lake complete with a whimsical grotto. Although she had often enjoyed the scenic beauty of the island, she had never considered the notion of actually visiting the lovely spot. Hardly surprising considering the fact she was terrified of water.

"The island?"

"Yes. My grandfather built the grotto upon the island for my grandmother so they could have a place of privacy. It is the one place upon Falcon Park that you have not yet visited."

Beatrice could not deny a desire to view the grotto. Especially now that she realized it had been built by a gentleman obviously devoted to his lady.

Still, there was a wretched amount of water to be passed over.

"But Mr. Humbly—" she began weakly, only to be overridden by a determined Gabriel.

"The vicar has already left to call upon his friend. It will be several hours before he returns."

"Oh."

He tilted his head to one side. "Does the notion not appeal to you, my dear?"

She gave a small lift of her hands. "I have never been upon a picnic."

A slow, potent smile curved his lips. "It is a treat not to be missed, I assure you."

Beatrice bit her bottom lip. She could not deny a large portion of her desired to give in to temptation. Surely it could not hurt to share a simple meal with her husband, she reasoned. It certainly did not mean she had forgotten the pain he had inflicted upon her.

Not giving herself time to ponder her peculiar logic, Beatrice gave a slow nod of her head.

"Very well."

Appearing suitably pleased by her capitulation, Gabriel moved forward to take her arm. He led her to the boat and with great care settled her upon the narrow seat. Then with a hard shove he pushed the boat into the water and leaped in to join her.

Beatrice felt her breath catch as they rocked precariously. Even after Gabriel had settled upon his seat and put the oars into motion, she continued to anticipate disaster.

The water was so very, very close. And it was such a great distance to the island. How could they possibly make it before they sank?

Unaware that her concern was clearly visible in her stiff frame, Beatrice was surprised when Gabriel gave a low chuckle.

"You needn't clutch the sides of the boat, Beatrice. I promise not to spill you into the water."

She grimaced although her fingers remained grimly attached to the boat.

"I have never felt comfortable in a boat. I suppose it is because I am unable to swim."

He flashed her a teasing glance. "Good heavens. I never thought to discover a skill you have not mastered."

"You are well aware that there are a great number of skills I have never mastered, much to the dismay of my mother," she retorted in jaundiced tones.

"I was not referring to the ridiculous accomplishments expected by society, but the true skills that are acquired by intelligence and genuine study."

Her gaze abruptly dropped. His words touched her far more deeply than she cared to admit.

"My studies never included paddling about in the water."

"That could easily be corrected. I will teach you to swim if you would care to learn."

Beatrice shuddered. Her fear of water was as unshakable as it was unreasonable.

"Thank you, but I prefer to be upon dry land."

"How do you know if you do not give it a try?"

She lifted her head to offer him a smile. "Just as I know I should not desire to leap from a cliff although I have never given it a try."

He gave a chuckle of defeat. "Very well, I shall not press you. How did you find Mrs. Litton?"

Relieved to have something to take her mind off the sound of water slapping against the boat, Beatrice turned her thoughts to her recent visit with the widow.

"Mending nicely, I am thankful to say. Her daughter will arrive tomorrow to care for her."

Not appearing to be tiring from his efforts at rowing, Gabriel shook his head ruefully.

"She is a shocking old tartar."

"She is certainly one to speak her mind," Beatrice agreed.

"No matter what is upon it."

"Yes." Beatrice abruptly recalled her conversation with the older woman. "In fact, she was telling me of the falcon's blessing."

He gave a startled blink. "Good gads, I had nearly forgotten that old tale."

"You are fortunate. I believe most families with such a long history are burdened with curses rather than blessings."

"I do not doubt that there are any number of curses

attached to the Faulconer name, but with our usual arrogance we choose to recall only the blessing," he retorted dryly.

"Far more convenient," she agreed.

"Indeed." The hazel gaze rested a long while upon her pale countenance. "And astonishingly dependable. There has yet to be a Countess of Faulconer who did not bring pride to the family name."

Once again Beatrice was forced to battle a childish blush. She was in no way out of the ordinary, she reminded herself. In truth, she possessed few of the skills expected in a countess. Her grandfather's merchant blood flowed far too strongly within her.

"Are you not rather tempting fate?" she muttered. "I might very well prove an end to the blessing."

He rewarded her offhand words with a sharp frown. "You are well aware that you are beloved among the tenants as well as the staff."

And by you?

The question was sternly squashed.

As was the dull ache in the region of her heart.

"Nonsense," she breathed in embarrassment.

"You are the one being nonsensical," he countered. "You are not perhaps fishing for compliments, are you, my dear?"

Her eyes widened with dismay. "Of course not."

"Then we shall simply agree that I could not have made a wiser choice when selecting my countess. Whether it was an extraordinary stroke of luck or an ancient blessing, we shall leave in the hands of the philosophers." He paused before allowing his features to soften with a hint of amusement. "By the bye, I suppose that Mrs. Litton was not nearly so flattering when it came to discussing the earls of Faulconer?"

She shifted with a hint of unease, for the moment forgetting the horrid water that surrounded her.

"Perhaps not your father," she conceded, knowing Gabriel would never believe that Mrs. Litton had spoken well of the previous earl. She had been his most outspoken critic for years. "But she could not speak well enough of you. She says that you have brought the tenants hope."

Surprisingly, Gabriel merely grimaced at the wholehearted praise. "I need to bring more than hope. What they are in need of is a bountiful planting season."

She gave a faint frown. "You have done what you could. Now it is in the hands of God."

"A rather daunting knowledge. I had not realized being an earl would entail such a great number of worries. I assure you that being a simple soldier was considerably less trying upon my nerves."

Beatrice did not doubt his sincerity. Unlike far too many earls, Gabriel fully shouldered his responsibilities. He did not dash about London while others struggled to provide him with luxuries. Instead, he gave of himself utterly. Whatever was demanded of his tenants, he expected even more of himself.

"Do you regret that you were forced to sell out?" she asked softly.

He took a moment to consider his answer. "I possessed no particular love for military life. It could be extraordinarily tedious as well as devilishly uncomfortable. Still, there was a measure of independence that greatly appealed to me."

"Yes." Beatrice nodded her head, all too familiar with the longing for liberty. "As a woman, there is little opportunity for true independence."

The hazel eyes narrowed. "Do you feel so oppressed, then, Beatrice?"

Surprisingly, Beatrice discovered she did not wish to continue their familiar battle.

"No, of course not. It is just frustrating to realize there are no options but being a burden to one's family or marrying."

A portion of his tension eased, but his gaze remained watchful.

"True enough. You would have been a brilliant businesswoman. Quite formidable, in fact."

She was caught off guard by the sincerity in his tone. "I should not say that."

"I would," he insisted. "Which is precisely why I wish to see you use your skills to their fullest advantage. There is no reason you cannot be a brilliant woman of business as well as Countess of Faulconer." He gave her no time to respond to his stunning pronouncement as he angled the boat toward the small dock. Tying off the rope, he stepped easily off the boat and reached down to help her alight. "Careful."

Startled to discover she had made the journey without mishap, Beatrice absently smoothed her wrinkled skirts. It was a small miracle that she hadn't panicked and sent them both into the water.

Gabriel bent downward to retrieve a large basket from the boat as Beatrice gazed at the lovely grotto fashioned in a classical style. Even the layout of the formal garden was still visible beneath the overgrowth with several small fountains surrounding the grotto.

"Oh, it is lovely," she said in pleasure.

"Yes, this is one of my favorite places upon the entire estate."

A pang that was perilously close to envy assaulted her heart.

"Your grandfather must have loved your grandmother very much."

"Yes, he was devoted to her. Unfortunately she was unable to conceive more than one child, and they spoiled my father shamelessly. Which no doubt accounts for his irresponsible habits and the belief he was due whatever pleasure he desired. Tendencies he readily passed on to my elder brother."

She slowly turned to meet his gaze. "But not you."

"No?" His lips twisted. "I have proven to be shockingly selfish and quite willing to lie when it suits my purpose."

Although Beatrice would have swiftly agreed with his derisive words only days before, at the moment she discovered herself reluctant to allow him to wholly condemn his desperate decisions.

Unlike his father and brother, he had not been entirely self-indulgent.

"For your tenants," she grudgingly muttered.

The hazel eyes darkened as a rueful smile curved his lips. "So I told myself." He took her hand and tugged her toward the narrow pathway. "We shall have our picnic in the grotto, although I cannot promise that it is in the best condition. I doubt that anyone has visited the island since I left Derbyshire."

"I assure you that I have become impervious to dust," she retorted wryly. Together they moved toward the grotto, but glancing over her shoulder, Beatrice came to an abrupt halt. "Oh."

"What is it?" Gabriel demanded.

Turning fully about, Beatrice regarded the proud silhouette of Falcon Park in the distance. Bathed in the late afternoon sunlight, it possessed a grand majesty. Even the sadly neglected parkland held a sweeping beauty.

"It is stunning."

Gabriel turned to stand beside her. "Yes. I used to mourn the fact that I could not paint. It would make a lovely landscape."

"Perhaps we should consider hiring an artist."

"A wonderful notion."

A smile suddenly curved Beatrice's lips. "It is a pity that Addy is not here. She would dearly appreciate such a vision. She was forever painting the houses and ruins about our neighborhood."

"Addy?" Gabriel queried with a lift of his brow.

Beatrice's smile widened as she thought of her vibrant, devil-may-care friend.

"I suppose I should say Mrs. Drake now. She was my very dearest friend growing up. Along with Victoria."

His expression became indulgent. "I suppose you were a precocious child?"

She gave a blink of surprise. "Not at all. I was very quiet and studious."

He tilted back his head to laugh with rich amusement. "Fah. You are too swift-witted and sharp-tongued to have been anything but precocious."

Her lips twitched in spite of herself. It was true that she had caused her share of trouble along with her friends.

"Perhaps a bit, but I assure you that it was nothing compared to either Addy or Victoria. They were far more daring than I."

He studied her reminiscent expression. "Why do you not invite them for a visit?"

"Oh . . ." She gave a flustered lift of her hands. She was uncertain that she wished her friends to realize what a terrible hash she had made of her marriage. "I do not know."

"Surely you would enjoy their company?"

"Perhaps later in the summer."

"As you wish," he murmured, perhaps sensing her reluctance to face her friends. With a faint sigh he held out his arm. "Shall we?"

Eight

Gabriel gave a faint grimace as they entered the shadowed mustiness of the grotto. Although it was thankfully dry, most of the delicate furnishings had been removed and only dust and cobwebs remained.

Perhaps it had not been such a brilliant notion after all, he wryly conceded.

When he had first pondered an appropriate place to have his wife to himself, the island had struck him as a perfect location. Not only would they be assured of their privacy, but there was a lingering sense of love that his grandparents had created.

Now he could only give a rueful sigh at his choice. They might be alone, but there was nothing romantic about sitting upon a hard floor with the threat of spiders lurking in the corners.

He had warned Humbly he possessed no hand at wooing women.

Still, there was nothing to do but attempt to make the best of the situation.

"Dear heavens, it is worse than I feared," he admitted with a glance toward his silent companion. "Are you game, or would you prefer to return to the house?"

She gave a faint shrug. "We have come this far. I do not propose to cry craven unless you wish to do so."

"Good girl," he complimented her with a smile. With

swift motions he spread a blanket upon the floor, then, waiting for Beatrice to take a seat, he settled close beside her and began to fill the plates with the large quantity of food that had been provided by Cook. "Ah, a veritable feast," he said, handing one of the full plates to Beatrice. "Here."

"Thank you." With a rather self-conscious manner she began delicately tasting the salmon in lobster sauce, beef, olives, potatoes, and fresh oranges.

Gabriel poured them both a glass of champagne before leaning back to regard his wife with a curious expression.

"Now, tell me more of your childhood."

She appeared startled by his command. "There is little to tell. In truth, it was all very dull."

"Indulge me," Gabriel insisted, wanting to know more of this woman he had made his countess. In far too many ways they were still virtually strangers. If he hoped to achieve a more intimate relationship, he realized he needed to know more of her hidden thoughts and feelings.

She paused before giving a lift of her hands. "I was fortunate in that my parents were very devoted to me."

"They were good parents?"

Her lips twisted. "As you know, they are beautiful, charming, and the darlings of society. You can imagine their confusion when they were given a daughter like me. They did their best, however, to hide their dismay."

Gabriel was not overly impressed. He had only briefly met his in-laws, but they had struck him as shallow nitwits who had no true comprehension of their daughter's unique qualities.

"Not well enough," he muttered.

She lifted her brows. "Whatever do you mean?"

"Being beautiful and charming or even the toast of society is all well and good, but possessing a kind and generous soul is far more commendable," he said in forceful tones. "That they allowed you to believe you were somehow lacking the finer qualities is reprehensible."

"Oh, no." She set aside her plate, her brow furrowed. "They never intended to make me feel as if I were lacking in anything. Indeed, they would be horrified if they thought I was in any way discomfitted. It was simply a matter of differing tastes. They enjoyed the glitter of London, while I preferred to remain in Surrey with my grandfather."

"They should have made more of a push to take an interest in you," he retorted.

"They did their best."

It was obvious that Beatrice could not accept that her parents had failed to provide her with the wholehearted approval she deserved. Gabriel wisely shifted the conversation to a happier topic.

"You at least had your grandfather."

Her expression predictably softened. "Yes. I do not believe that I was ever so happy as when we were together in his workshop. Mama thought him eccentric and something of an embarrassment, for he was forever attired in grubby clothing with dust upon his face. She claimed he appeared more of a farmhand than a wealthy man of business."

Gabriel gave a soft chuckle. "Having spent several weeks as a farmhand, I find nothing offensive in grubby clothes and dust upon a person's countenance. I have had far worse upon my own."

Casting a rueful glance down at her own stained gown, Beatrice wrinkled her nose.

"Clearly I have no aversion to dust and whatnot myself."

Shifting even closer, Gabriel allowed his gaze to linger

over the lush curves that had been driving him to distraction.

"We are well matched, it seems."

He could see her battle the sudden crackle of awareness that sparked to life between them.

"Yes, well, unfortunately my grandfather died and I reached the age I could no longer ignore my parents' demands that I present myself in London."

"A hideous fate, eh?" he teased, discovering it incredibly difficult to concentrate upon their conversation. The need to possess this woman was swiftly becoming a fever in his blood. Never could he recall desiring a woman with such force.

"Fairly hideous," she retorted, her own breath uneven.

"You were not alone in your misery, you know," he murmured softly. "I cannot conceive the lure of spending weeks upon weeks enduring that choking black air, the cluttered streets, and overdressed fops. Even worse were the crowded ballrooms where a gentleman could not take a step without being latched on to by some matchmaking mama. Gads, I still have nightmares about my brief stay."

She appeared remarkably unsympathetic to the trial he had endured.

"You were there only a few weeks; I was forced to remain for three Seasons."

"My sympathies," he swiftly consoled her, then, noting the sudden frown that tugged at her brows, he leaned forward. "What is it?"

"Nothing." She attempted to dismiss her concern.

"Beatrice."

She gave a restless shrug. "I was just thinking that had I had my way, I would have been in Surrey rather than London and we should never have met."

Gabriel could not prevent his sudden scowl.

Never to have met Beatrice?

It was unthinkable.

Surely she had been destined to become Countess of Faulconer?

To be his wife?

To even consider another was unbearable.

He was briefly shaken by the stark intensity of his reaction to her words. As well as by the realization that Beatrice clearly shared no similar sense of fate.

"Yet another reason to detest London, eh, my dear?" he said, his tone more harsh than he had intended.

A faint color touched her cheeks. "No doubt for you as well. Had I not been available you would have found another heiress who would have been far more amenable than I."

He did not doubt for a moment than any number of women would have been more amenable. Indeed, he would be hard pressed not to find another who was more amenable than Beatrice.

Unfortunately, not one of them had done more than bore him senseless within a few moments.

"Unlike you, I do not regret our marriage. Indeed, I become more convinced each passing day I could not have made a better choice."

Her lashes abruptly lowered over her eyes, as if seeking to hide her inner thoughts.

"You did not wish to marry for love?"

Gabriel briefly considered her question. He had rarely thought of marriage. Without hope for an inheritance and destined for a career in the military, he had precious little to offer a maiden. And in truth, after his own childhood, a family seemed far more a burden than a blessing.

It was only after Beatrice had arrived at Falcon Park that he had discovered a restless urge to build more than a chilled partnership. He wanted the bonds of genuine friendship. And perhaps someday, if God willed it so, children to call his own.

"It is difficult to desire what you have never known," he said carefully. "Certainly my parents possessed no feelings for each other. Even those acquaintances of mine who wed for so-called love more often than not became swiftly disillusioned and realized too late such a fickle emotion is a treacherous basis for marriage. Surely it is best to search for a partner you respect and truly enjoy spending time with?"

She absently plucked at a ribbon upon her gown. "My parents have always possessed a great love for each other. A love that has only strengthened over time."

Gabriel grimaced as he realized that beneath Beatrice's brisk competency was a heart that ached for love. A love that she had no doubt hoped she had found in him.

Damn.

Would reminders of his treachery never end?

"I suppose every marriage is as different as the people who say their vows," he said gently. "We have a great deal between us to build a strong relationship."

Her gaze abruptly lifted in surprise. "I would say we have very little between us."

"We both care for Falcon Park," he pointed out in reasonable tones.

"I suppose." She was forced to concede.

"We both prefer the country to London," he continued. "Neither of us suffers fools gladly, and we both have our own interests so that we are not constantly tripping over each other."

She smiled wryly at his imminent logic. "Preferring to go our own way and disliking fools is not precisely the stuff the poets spout about."

Gabriel was not about to be put off. Not when he was quite convinced that they were so well suited.

"Perhaps not, but admit, Beatrice, that you would be miserable with an overbearing husband who demanded your constant attention and refused to allow you to follow your own interests."

She bit her lip as if debating whether to lie or admit the truth of his words. Then, clearly realizing she could not deceive him, she gave a lift of her shoulders.

"As you say."

Her grudging concession sent a surge of annoyance through him. Blast it all. Why could she not give in the slightest? For better or worse, they were wed.

Surely she could see it was best to seek what happiness was possible?

What pleasure was possible?

Needing to prove the truth by the only means available, Gabriel determinedly leaned forward. Beatrice could deny the rightness of their being together with her words, but could she resist the power of the need that smoldered between them?

He had to discover if she could.

With a slow motion he reached up to pluck the straw hat from her curls, nonchalantly tossing it aside.

Her lips parted in surprise. "Gabriel."

"Yes, Beatrice?" he murmured as he shifted to place one hand on each side of her hips and regarded those temptingly parted lips.

"What are you doing?"

"Making you a bit more comfortable."

"I am perfectly comfortable, thank you," she choked out.

"Good." He bent to lightly brush her mouth with his own. "So am I."

"Gabriel."

He gently nuzzled the corner of her mouth. "I am merely attempting to assure you that we have more in common than you are willing to admit."

She stiffened at his soft caress, but much to his satisfaction, she did not push him away.

"I do not think this is wise," she breathed.

"Do not think, my dear, merely feel," he urged, angling his head to claim her lips in a seeking kiss.

Heady sweetness swept through him as her lips softened beneath his own. Gads, this was what he had dreamed of night after long night. The feel of her satin lips, the poignant excitement of her hesitant response. Even the faint honeysuckle scent that clung to her skin had invaded his dreams.

A sharp hunger filled him as he lifted his hand to cup the back of her neck. She felt perfect in his arms. So warm, so utterly soft. So tempting.

She trembled, and Gabriel grimly forced himself to ignore the urge to press her backward and allow the passion to sweep over them.

She might be his wife, but she was an innocent. He would not frighten her or steal her pleasure by rushing her.

Easing his lips, he lightly nibbled down the length of her jaw. Her skin was as smooth as the finest silk, and he explored it with fascinated pleasure. From her jaw he moved to the delicate curve of her neck, where he lingered upon the frantic beat of her pulse.

He smiled at the instinctive reaction she could not hide behind her icy indifference. Whatever her anger and disappointment, she still desired his touch. It was not enough, but surely it was something to build upon.

Careful not to startle her, Gabriel allowed his hands to shift to her back, pulling her closer to his aching body. She gasped as her curves were pressed to the hard muscles, but her hands clutched convulsively at his shoulders. His lips returned to her mouth, deepening the kiss with an increasing urgency. He did not wish to frighten her, but the demands of his own body were swiftly taking control.

He wanted this woman.

He ached, trembled, and burned for this woman.

It would have been a frightening knowledge if he were capable of thinking in a rational manner.

Never before had he allowed his desires to consume him. Never before had a woman managed to lodge herself so firmly beneath his fierce self-control.

At the moment, however, there was nothing rational about his thoughts. There was just the delicious warmth of the woman in his arms.

Tentatively touching the curve of her lip with his tongue, Gabriel was vaguely aware of a scraping noise above his head. He paid it no heed as he traced the quivering outline of her mouth. But when it came again with more force than before, Beatrice was determinedly pulling away and regarding him with dazed eyes.

"What was that?" she whispered.

Gabriel did not particularly give a grout, but realizing Beatrice would not relax until he discovered the cause for the ill-timed noise, he forced his stiff body upright and moved to the edge of the grotto.

What he discovered brought a scowl to his countenance.

Bloody hell.

While he had been so enwrapped with Beatrice, he had failed to notice the building bank of clouds that now completely blocked the sun. Lightning abruptly streaked through the air, and a sharp breeze tugged at the nearby trees, causing them to scrape against the tiles of the grotto.

Well, he had discovered the cause of the noise, along with the knowledge he had effectively trapped Beatrice upon the island until the storm had passed.

No doubt the grotto leaked, the wind would blow straight through the loose boards, and they would both be wet and freezing before it was said and done.

He heaved a rueful sigh. He doubted his wife, or any woman for that matter, would be pleased with the sudden turn of events.

So much for his attempt at romance. He truly had no talent for it.

Turning about, he discovered Beatrice on her feet with the familiar wary expression.

He sighed again. It appeared any hope for a satisfying conclusion to his seduction was at an end.

"The wind appears to have stiffened," he explained as he moved toward the center of the grotto.

"Perhaps we should return to the house."

He shook his head. "I think we had best remain until the storm passes."

"Oh, but—"

"Beatrice." He reached out to lightly clasp her shoulders. "If you disliked the lake when it was perfectly still, you are bound to dislike it even more now."

As Beatrice glanced toward the lake, which had turned a dark gray with choppy waves, her face paled.

"Yes."

"There is nothing to do but to remain here for the time being," he said briskly.

She swallowed heavily. "I suppose."

Reaching down, Gabriel swiftly repacked the basket and retrieved the blanket.

"Let us move to the back of the grotto. We do not wish to be drenched when the rain arrives." He steered her toward the back and placed her on a stone bench. Then carefully he draped the blanket over her knees before settling beside her. "Now, it appears we shall have to keep ourselves entertained for quite some time. Do you have any suggestions, my dear?"

A flush warmed her skin at his suggestive tone, but her expression was primly disapproving.

"We could discuss the renovations on Falcon Park."

Gabriel grimaced. "A rather tedious subject."

"Would you prefer to discuss the planting season?"

He lifted his hand to lightly stroke the curve of her cheek.

"I would prefer to discuss how very soft your skin feels beneath my fingers. And how those lips are driving me to madness."

Her breath quickened. "Gabriel."

"I want you, Beatrice," he said in husky tones.

The magnificent amber eyes darkened. "Because you need an heir?"

Gabriel froze, his hand falling away in furious disbelief. "What did you say?"

She licked her suddenly dry lips.

"I realize that you must think of the future. As Earl of Faulconer, you must have a son."

"Bloody hell." Gabriel rose to his feet and glared down at her stubborn expression. "You give me a good deal of credit to be able to command my body to respond upon demand. And absolutely no credit for the smallest claim to morals."

She flinched at his sharp words, but her gaze remained disbelieving.

"You do not think of an heir when you kiss me?"

He shoved his hands through his hair. It was that or grasping her and shaking some sense into her thick skull.

Perhaps he should tell her precisely what he was thinking when he kissed her, he thought savagely. That in his deepest dreams she was not a sharp-tongued shrew, but the shy, uncertain girl he had courted. That instead of freezing when he neared, she opened her arms to him and pulled him atop those lush curves. That she softly moaned as he caressed that tender skin and cried out in pleasure when he at last took her.

He grimly reined in the fantasies that threatened to torture his body all over again.

"I damn well do not," he at last rasped.

"I am not beautiful," she perversely argued.

He flashed her a disgusted glance. "You know nothing of gentlemen if you believe a pretty countenance is all that makes a woman desirable. I have known any number of Incomparables who have not stirred the least amount of interest."

Her gaze refused to waver. "Then why do gentlemen pursue them with such determination?"

Gad, but she was an innocent, he acknowledged wryly.

"To be envied by the *ton*. I assure you that a gentleman who is seeking true passion searches for a woman of warmth and generosity. Not an icy beauty more concerned with her appearance than sharing a deep intimacy." He regarded her with a hint of regret. "You once offered such warmth. It still flows within you."

Her head abruptly dipped, as if seeking to hide her expressive countenance.

"I cannot deny that you are capable of making me respond to your touch."

His lips twisted at her reluctant tone. "Is that such a terrible thing? Most women would be well pleased to feel such desire for their husbands. I assure you that it is not always so."

He saw a tremble shake her body. "I no longer trust such emotions."

"Yes." Gabriel clutched his hands at his sides, a feeling of helpless frustration washing through him. "That is what keeps us apart, is it not? What must I do to regain your trust, Beatrice?"

"I do not know," she answered slowly.

"Then we are destined to be forever at odds."

"Gabriel—" Her words abruptly halted as she lifted her head. "What was that?"

Gabriel, too, had heard the ominous sound of splintering wood. It took a moment to realize that it came from directly overhead. A shaft of pure fear shot through him, and in a heartbeat he was rushing forward.

"Beatrice," he bellowed, throwing himself atop her even as the roof came crashing down.

Nine

Confusion held a firm upper hand.

Beatrice heard Gabriel's shout, then suddenly he was atop her and the entire world seemed to be descending upon them.

With the breath knocked from her body, it took Beatrice a considerable time to untangle herself from the sharp branches and crushed bits of the grotto that covered her. Gasping for breath and wiping the dirt from her stinging eyes, she gazed about in horror.

It was obvious that the wind had ripped off a large branch from a nearby tree, sending it crashing through the roof. A gaping hole overhead allowed the torrential rain to pour down upon them while lightning ripped through the air. But she paid no heed to the storm that suddenly raged about her. Instead, she fell to her knees to regard the man firmly trapped beneath the heavy branch.

"Gabriel," she choked, her heart faltering at the deep gash in his forehead that was sending blood flowing over his unnaturally pale countenance. "Dear Lord, Gabriel."

She nearly fainted with relief when his lashes fluttered slowly upward.

"Beatrice?"

"Thank heavens," she breathed, suddenly realizing that she had feared him dead. "Are you badly hurt?"

He paused a moment to take stock of his form still buried beneath branches and a heavy beam from the roof.

"I do not believe I have actually broken anything, although my head appears to be spinning."

Beatrice was not at all reassured by his weak tones. Whatever he might claim, it was obvious he was hurt.

She could not begin to surmise how badly.

"You have a terrible gash upon your forehead," she said softly.

He attempted to grimace, only to wince in pain. "I was afraid of that."

"Do you think you can move?"

Briefly closing his eyes, Gabriel concentrated on wiggling from beneath the heavy beam. It was obvious within moments, however, he was far too weak to make the effort.

"Bloody hell. It appears that I am stuck."

Beatrice sat back on her heels.

She had to think.

With an effort she attempted to still her near panic. Gabriel was clearly in no condition to decide what was to be done. It fell upon her to save them from this devilish predicament.

Glancing about the ruined grotto, she swiftly concluded they could not remain where they were. Not only were they exposed to the heavy rain falling from the heavens, there was no telling when another branch or even an entire tree might crash in upon them.

Unfortunately the beam was far too heavy for her to move. And there was no means to release Gabriel from beneath the wreckage.

"I must go for help," she concluded aloud.

Gabriel gave a brief, futile struggle against an imprisoning limb.

"Beatrice, no."

She frowned down at him, a sick dread in her stomach as the gash continued to ooze blood down his wet face.

"But you cannot remain in these damp clothes. You will surely catch a chill. And a doctor must see to that gash."

"Do not fear," he rasped. "Once we are missed, they will come to rescue us."

"But that might be hours," she protested.

"Then we will wait."

"That is absurd. You will be frozen."

With obvious effort he glared at her, a commanding expression in his eyes.

"Beatrice, I will not allow you to get into that boat on your own. It is far, far too dangerous."

Beatrice determinedly refused to contemplate the upcoming trip across the storm-tossed lake. She could not allow her ridiculous fear to paralyze her. Not when Gabriel's very life hung in the balance.

She would not allow him to die.

Not even if she had to take that bloody boat to the netherworld and back.

Somehow she managed to force a stiff smile to her lips. "You are hardly in a position to halt me."

"No." His lashes fluttered as if he were struggling to remain conscious. Beatrice felt her heart squeeze with a near-unbearable pain. "I utterly forbid it."

She reached out to gently stroke the wet hair from his forehead.

"Please be still, Gabriel. You will do yourself further harm."

"Promise me you will not try to return to the house," he whispered, his eyes closing as the weakness overtook him.

Dear Lord, please do not let him die, she inwardly

prayed, unwitting tears combining with the rain to pour down her cheeks.

"Gabriel."

He gave a deep moan. "Beatrice?"

"I am here."

"Stay with me," he muttered.

"All will be well," she retorted, firmly rising to her feet. She could not delay.

Already she could see Gabriel shivering with cold and the gash continued to bleed.

Even now his very life might be slipping from his body. She bit back a sob.

No.

She could not think in such a manner.

She had to concentrate on what must be done.

Grimly gathering her shattered nerves, Beatrice moved to retrieve the blanket. She carefully arranged it over the unconscious form of Gabriel, hoping it would protect him from the worst of the rain.

Then, not giving herself the opportunity to ponder what she was about to do, Beatrice left the grotto and made her way down to the boat.

Stoically, she placed one foot before the other, reassuring herself that the wind had significantly lessened and that the lightning was growing farther and farther away. It was not until she actually reached the boat that she faltered.

"You can do this, Beatrice," she told herself. "Just a few moments and you will be on land." A shudder racked her body. "You have to do this," she muttered. "Gabriel might very well die if you do not."

It was the mere thought of Gabriel dying that propelled her into the rocking boat and groping to undo the rope.

Gabriel would not die.

The very thought was unbearable.

It could not happen.

She would surely die herself.

Refusing to ponder the certainty of her demise without Gabriel, Beatrice clutched the oars and set them in awkward motion. Terror gripped her as water splashed over the sides and the boat tipped precariously.

Think of Gabriel, she sternly told herself. She had to get to the house. She had to get help.

She chanted the words over and over throughout the nightmare journey.

In time she forgot the grasping waves that sought to suck her under, the rain whipping against her, and even the fact that she was biting her lower lip hard enough to draw blood. All she could concentrate upon was the burning weariness that radiated from her shoulders and down her arms.

More than once she feared her arms would give out altogether. Despite the fact that she was a strong, physically active woman, the battle against the wind and waves was nearly overwhelming.

When she finally hit the shore, it came almost as a shock. For a moment she simply sat in the boat, shaking with exhaustion. She was far from certain she could move a weary muscle.

Then the memory of Gabriel lying unconscious, blood running down his face, sent a fresh wave of desperation through her. She had come too far to give up now.

Trembling from head to toe, Beatrice crawled out of the boat and battled her way through the mud. She fell more than once, but with sheer stubborn will she at last arrived at the house and pushed open the door to the foyer.

"Hello . . ." she called, her voice oddly hoarse.

It carried far enough, however, to bring the house-keeper, butler, and several footmen dashing to her side.

"My lady, we have been so concerned," Mrs. Greene cried.

"Please, there has been an accident," she said as she clutched the door for support.

The older woman gave a shriek of dismay. "Heaven have mercy. Is it Lord Faulconer?"

"Yes. I—"

Beatrice's words were cut short as the round form of Vicar Humbly hurried to her side.

"Beatrice, my child, what has occurred?"

"Lord Faulconer is on the island. A branch fell through the grotto and he is pinned beneath it."

The vicar's face paled. "He isn't . . . ?"

"No," Beatrice breathed, fiercely willing it so. "He is wounded but alive. I could not move him. I must have help."

"Of course." With a surprising efficiency, Humbly turned to regard the gathered servants. "You there." He pointed to a footman. "Gather two grooms from the stables and take the boat to the grotto. Be sure you do not jostle his lordship more than necessary. Oh, and take a few blankets with you to keep him warm." He pointed toward another footman. "You run and fetch the nearest doctor. Do not let him fob you off with some excuse of storms and muddy roads. Tell him that his lordship is injured and if he is not treated with all swiftness, it will be known throughout England he was failed by the local sawbones."

"Yes, sir."

The servants rushed to do his bidding, obviously eager to be of service to their beloved earl. Mrs. Greene abruptly straightened her shoulders.

"I must make some tea and some nice warm soup. The poor man will be chilled to the bone."

She disappeared down the hall, closely followed by the gaunt butler, who was muttering about a stash of brandy hidden in the cellars.

Beatrice would have been stunned by the bumbling vicar's sudden air of command if she hadn't been battling the most absurd need to sink to the floor.

As if sensing her distress, Humbly regarded her with a piercing gaze.

"I fear Lord Faulconer is not the only one chilled to the bone. Come, my dear, you must go upstairs and have a nice, hot bath."

With her teeth chattering, Beatrice gave a firm shake of her head.

"No, I must return to the island with the servants."

"Nonsense. You will catch your death of cold in those wet clothes."

"Gabriel needs me."

Humbly regarded her steadily. "I am quite certain that he does, which is why you must have a care for you own health. You will be of little use to him laid up for weeks with an inflammation of the lungs."

She stubbornly clung to the door, unable to bear the thought of not being at Gabriel's side.

"But—"

"Beatrice, the servants are much better suited to return Gabriel to the house," the vicar said firmly, taking a hold of her arm and tugging her toward the stairs. "Besides which, you would only be in the way once they have him in the boat."

"I cannot just wait," she protested as she discovered herself ruthlessly steered across the foyer.

"You will not be waiting. You will be taking a hot bath, followed by a large dose of brandy. You will then attire yourself in your warmest gown and be prepared to speak with the doctor."

Beatrice wanted to argue. It was her duty to be beside Gabriel. More than that, she needed to be beside Gabriel.

But a glimmer of common sense at last pierced her foggy terror.

She was so weary, she doubted she could make her way back to the lake, not without a servant carrying her. In such a condition she would be of no help to Gabriel. And as Humbly had pointed out, she would surely be in the way once they managed to load him into the boat.

Surely it would be better to regain her strength and be preparing for Gabriel's return?

"I suppose you are being sensible," she sighed.

He kindly patted her hand. "Most certainly I am. Now go. I will await the doctor here."

Gabriel regarded the small, nearly bald-headed gentleman with a jaundiced glare. He had not liked the look of that weasel face from the moment he had walked into the room. He liked him even less after a quarter of an hour of being poked, prodded, and kneaded like he was a lump of dough rather than a nobly born gentleman.

Luckily for the weasel-faced man, he was feeling as if he had been run over by a team of oxen. Otherwise he would have picked him up by those protruding ears and tossed him out the nearest window long ago.

As if able to read his dark thoughts, the demonic doctor found the most tender spot upon his ribs and dug his finger in with a ruthless force.

"Bloody hell," Gabriel yelped in pain. "For how long do you intend to poke at me in that rude fashion?"

Straightening, the small man offered him a prunish

frown. "I must ascertain you have no further injuries beyond a cut on the head."

Scooting on the bed until he was out of ready reach of his tormentor, Gabriel pulled the blanket up to his chin. After losing consciousness beneath the branch the previous evening, he had no awareness of what had occurred until he had awakened this morning with a raging headache and this wretched doctor hovering above him like an angel of death.

All he wanted was a hot bath, a large dose of brandy, and, most of all, to see Beatrice and assure himself she had not caught a chill as they had waited to be rescued.

"I have told you I am quite well," he growled in exasperation.

The weasel lips thinned. "And perhaps you would care to tell me precisely when you attended the Royal College of Physicians?"

Gabriel gave a snort. "I should know whether I sustained a life-threatening wound. It is my body, after all."

"Would you care to know how many buffleheaded patients have gone to meet their maker while swearing they were perfectly fit?"

Buffleheaded?

Why the pompous, twittering fool.

"More likely it was from your poking," he muttered, only to wince as the man reached out to prod his thigh. "Ow. You did that on purpose."

A smug smile touched the weasel countenance. "Never argue with the doctor."

"Tormentor, more like."

The doctor straightened and placed his hands on his hips. "Would you prefer I leave an elixir for you?"

Gabriel shuddered in horror. "You wouldn't."

"Without the least pang of remorse. I have a particularly nasty one that I leave with patients like you."

"Devil," Gabriel accused. "Be off with you."

"Gabriel?"

The softly questioning voice had Gabriel turning his head to discover Beatrice standing in the doorway. A rush of relief flooded through him as he noted her yellow gown as yet unstained by her numerous activities and the soft honey hair piled atop her head. In the morning sunlight she looked fresh and utterly healthy. Thank God, she had no seeming effects from the horrid incident.

"My dear, thank goodness you are here," he said, holding out his hand toward her.

With a faint frown she hurried forward, surprisingly taking the hand he offered between both of her own.

"Is something the matter?"

"Nothing other than the fact that this demon is determined to bruise me from head to toe."

The doctor gave a loud sniff. "Lady Faulconer, may I tell you that never has it been my honor to serve such an ill-tempered, thick-skulled gentleman?"

Beatrice glanced toward Gabriel with a lift of her brows. "I presume he refuses to allow you to examine him?"

"He is being most uncooperative."

"Really, Gabriel," she chided.

"I am fine."

"You have a very nasty wound upon your head and several deep bruises. They should heal in time, but only if you remain in bed and behave in a sensible manner."

Beatrice firmly drew her hand from Gabriel's fingers as she sent him a speaking glance.

"You need not concern yourself, Doctor. I shall ensure that he behaves in a sensible fashion."

"See that you do." The doctor closed his bag with a snap and collected his hat and gloves. "If I am forced to return, I will not only prescribe an elixir, I will have him bled until he is too weak to behave like a stubborn child. Good day."

Having delivered his dire warning, the doctor grandly swept from the room.

Gabriel grimaced as he silently wished the man good riddance.

"Buffoon," he muttered.

Beatrice clicked her tongue at his petulant tone. "Really, Gabriel, you are behaving like a child."

He wondered how she would feel if she were the one being gouged. No doubt she would have boxed the doctor's ears.

"I do not wish to be confined to my bed like an elderly invalid."

"It is only for a few days. Surely you would not wish to do yourself further injury?"

He gave an impatient shake of his head, only to moan in pain.

Blast it all.

"I have too much to do to lie here."

Obviously noting his unwitting wince, Beatrice's expression hardened.

"There is nothing that the tenants and your steward cannot attend to."

"But I wished to begin work on your new office," he complained.

Her expression remained disobliging. "The work can wait a week or two."

"And what of our guest?"

"I will see to Vicar Humbly's comfort."

Gads, did she have to be so devilishly practical, he unjustly stewed.

"And what of my comfort?" he grumbled. "Who will see to that?"

A reluctant smile suddenly twitched at her lips. "You are a remarkably petulant invalid, Gabriel."

Realizing he was indeed behaving like a spoiled twit, Gabriel heaved a rueful sigh.

He had no right to take his ill humor out on Beatrice. She was only attempting to make him be sensible.

"Forgive me, my dear. It is only that I dislike feeling helpless."

She gave a slow nod of her head, her eyes darkening. "I am deeply relieved that your injuries will heal. When I left you on the island, I was uncertain—"

"You left me on the island?" Gabriel felt an icy chill grip his body as he glared at his suddenly flustered wife. "Do not tell me that you took that boat out in the midst of a storm?"

"Yes, well, the storm had all but passed, and I could not allow you to remain trapped beneath that branch."

Gabriel had not been so furious in his entire life. Not when he had discovered that his father had utterly ruined the estate. Not when the tenants had treated him as if he were some loathsome being who was about to snatch away the last of their meager belongings. Not even when Beatrice had turned from him in icy disgust.

To even consider the notion of Beatrice alone in that blasted boat when the smallest wave could have sent her tumbling to her death! God, it crushed his heart to even allow such a hideous thought enter his mind.

"I had expressly forbidden you to go," he said between clenched teeth. "Good God, you could have been drowned."

"I took great care, I assure you. Better care than you took in thrusting me aside and endangering yourself."

He gripped the blanket tightly. It was that or reaching out to grasp the overly stubborn, nit-witted woman.

"If I were not feeling as weak as a bloody kitten, I

should put you over my knee. How dare you do something so idiotic? I shall have nightmares for years thinking of you on that lake."

She shook her head, sending a handful of silken curls tumbling about her face.

"As you can see, I am perfectly well."

His gaze ran a heated path over her flushed countenance and the manner her fingers nervously plucked at the lace upon her gown. His anger abruptly faded as a wrenching tenderness flooded through him.

"Dash it all. Why?" he demanded with a searching gaze. "Why did you do such a thing?"

She awkwardly turned to pace toward the window, effectively hiding her expression from his piercing regard.

"Because I was terrified you were seriously injured. And just as important, I could not allow you to remain in those damp clothes. It might have been several hours before we were missed. Or they might not have thought to search for us upon the island. I had to do something."

He gave a low growl deep in his throat. "But you risked your life."

"It was no more than you did," she said in low tones.

"Fah."

She slowly turned to face him. "If you had not pushed me aside, I should have been hit by that branch."

Gabriel grimaced, not at all willing to be named a hero. "If I had not induced you to go to that wretched island in the first place, neither of us would have been in danger."

Without warning, a smile suddenly lightened her countenance. It was that smile that had first drawn him across the crowded London ballroom to seek an introduction, he abruptly recalled. It was filled with such genuine sweetness. Such purity of spirit. It had called out to his battered and cynical soul with the lure of a siren.

Now he felt his entire body respond to the warmth of that smile.

"Do you mean to say you cannot predict the future?" she teased with a lift of her brows. "A most shocking failure, my lord. Most shocking."

He returned her smile, but there was a grim resolution that ran through him.

Never again would he allow Beatrice to be in such danger.

He would gladly lay down his life before he would allow her to be harmed.

"I promise to take much better care of you in the future, my dear," he said fiercely.

Her fingers returned to pluck at her lace as their gazes entangled.

Gabriel abruptly recalled their heated embrace that had been so rudely interrupted. Just for a moment she had been as lost in passion as himself, he acknowledged. They had been so very close to utter paradise. Would she ever allow herself to lower her defenses again?

"You will not be doing anything for the next few days," she at last forced herself to say.

Gabriel deliberately allowed the blanket to slip downward, revealing a portion of his bare chest. A tingling pleasure replaced his groggy pain as he heard her breath catch.

"Now, that brings up an interesting dilemma," he said in husky tones.

She swallowed heavily. "What is that?"

He raised his arms to pillow them behind his head. "You faithfully promised that horrid doctor to keep me in bed. I should very much like to discover precisely how you intend to achieve such a feat."

A delightful flush heated her face, but her chin tilted upward.

"Perhaps I shall have you tied to the posts."

He gave a low, seductive chuckle. "I have a much better notion, my sweet Beatrice."

"And what is that?"

"Come closer and I'll tell you."

Her eyes widened as his low laughter filled the room.

Ten

Beatrice was perfectly aware that Gabriel was teasing her. Even across the room she could see the devilish glint in the hazel eyes. But after the desperate panic of the day before, followed by the sheer relief of realizing Gabriel would soon recover, she discovered her icy composure decidedly absent.

Instead, she felt a flustered heat fill her cheeks.

"Really, Gabriel."

He lifted his brows. Lying against the pillows with his hands tucked behind his head and an indecent amount of his bare chest exposed, he appeared utterly at ease. Quite unlike herself. She was stiff and wary as the prickly awareness became more pronounced.

"What, Beatrice?" he demanded in low tones.

She licked her lips, belatedly wishing she had pretended to misunderstand his words. She possessed no talent for this dangerous banter.

"You are injured." She blurted out the first words that came to mind.

His low laugh seemed to reach out and stroke over her skin.

"The blow to my head did not damage my memories. I can still clearly recall the feel of you in my arms. And the fact that nothing has ever felt so wonderful before."

She attempted to appear stern, although she feared that she more closely resembled an awkward schoolgirl.

"I am quite certain such thoughts cannot be good for you in your condition."

"I will admit that my condition is a painful one," he agreed, allowing his gaze to run a warm path over her curves. "But you are the cause of that, not some wayward branch."

Her breath caught. He was not the only one with poignant memories of their embrace. She could vividly recall each kiss, each warm caress of his hands. She could also recall how she had seemed to melt with burning need. The faint ache still remained deep within her.

"You are attempting to embarrass me."

"Not at all." His eyes narrowed. "Why should you be embarrassed by a perfectly natural emotion? We are man and wife."

"Yes, but . . ."

"But you believe that I am merely plotting the means of producing my heirs without resorting to actual force?"

Beatrice shifted uneasily.

Saints above. Why had she ever confessed her inner doubts? It was obvious that he was overreacting to her distrust. She had never thought him a monster.

"Of course not."

"It is what you accused me of only yesterday."

She could hardly deny the words that had come from her own lips. Instead, she gave a restless shrug.

"I have had reason to distrust your motives in regard to me."

He slowly lowered his arms and regarded her with a somber expression.

"Beatrice, I might have concealed my need for wealth, but I never pretended my true regard for you. It is as genuine as my desire to build Falcon Park into an estate you will be proud to call home. And I certainly never pretended when I promised to be a good husband to you. All I wish is to see you happy again."

It was so tempting to accept his low words. In truth, Beatrice was weary of being angry. And since Vicar Humbly's arrival, she had begun to wonder if she was indeed indulging in a fit of spiteful retaliation just as the older man had accused.

After all, Gabriel had done his best to be a good husband since they had arrived in Derbyshire. Unlike most gentlemen, he had been extraordinarily patient with her. Not only by not insisting upon his rights to her bed, but by giving her full control of restoring the household, and, of course, encouraging her interest in inventions. What other man would have been so generous?

Still, she discovered herself unable to wholly dismiss her lingering distrust.

Her heart was too tender to risk another blow. She simply could not bear it.

"I wish to be happy," she grudgingly confessed.

His features abruptly softened. "Then allow me to be your husband, Beatrice."

"You mean to welcome you to my bed?" she demanded warily.

He smiled in a rueful fashion. "I will not lie, my sweet, I certainly desire to be in your bed. But that is only a small portion of being a proper husband. I wish a share in your life."

"A share in my life?"

"I wish to know about your inventions, your frustrations in restoring the house, your visits to the tenants. I wish to know what has made you laugh during the day and if something has made you sad. I want you to turn to me if there is something you need."

His words touched a vulnerable place deep within her.

A place that had always longed for such closeness with another. Instinctively she found herself retreating.

"I would bore you senseless," she quipped lightly.

"Do not, Beatrice," he said sternly. "This is too important to be dismissed."

She caught her bottom lip between her teeth. He was right. This was too important. Their very future hung in the balance.

"I do not know if I am yet prepared, Gabriel."

He smiled kindly and held out his hand. "Come here, my dear."

She hesitated only a moment before crossing the room and placing her hand in his warm fingers.

"Yes?"

He gave her hand a small squeeze, but when she gasped suddenly, he turned her palm upward to regard the raw wounds she had nearly forgotten.

"Good God, what have you done to yourself?" he demanded in shock.

"I . . . nothing."

He stabbed her with a frown. "This is not nothing."

"I suppose it is from pulling the oars," she reluctantly confessed.

"Of course." He heaved a harsh sigh. "Do you have any further injuries that you have attempted to hide from me?"

"My shoulders are a trifle sore, but nothing else."

"My poor Beatrice." He tenderly lifted her hand to place a kiss upon her palm. The flare of warmth arced all the way to the pit of her stomach. "I had intended to sweep you off your feet and instead I nearly got you killed."

"You are hardly responsible for the storm, nor the branch that crashed upon us. It was a simple matter of ill luck."

"Forgive me," he muttered, kissing her fingers, then stroking a path back down to the sensitive skin of her wrist.

Quite certain she was about to collapse onto the bed as heat flooded through her body, Beatrice struggled to focus her wayward thoughts.

"You are being absurd, Gabriel, there is nothing to forgive."

"At the very least, I should be forgiven for making such a botch of our picnic."

"There will be other picnics."

"I do hope so." Those tantalizing lips skillfully circled her wrist, sending a searing path of excitement up her arm. "There are some parts that I remember quite fondly."

"Gabriel," she breathed.

He lightly nibbled at her knuckles. "Yes, my dear?"

"You must take care."

"I am attempting to take great care." He lifted his head to reveal the wicked glint in his eye. "Do you approve?"

Oh, she approved, she inwardly acknowledged. How could she not? His soft caresses had set her entire body alight with shimmering pleasure.

But this was hardly the time for such intimate advances, she reluctantly lectured herself. Not only was Gabriel wounded, there was no predicting when a servant might suddenly enter the chambers.

She hardly wished to be caught being made love to by her husband in the middle of the morning. It was surely indecent.

With a determination she was far from feeling, Beatrice pulled her hand free.

"I must meet with the workmen."

His gaze searched her guarded features. "It cannot wait?"

"No . . . I . . . there is some question as to the exact lay-out of the rose garden."

There was a moment's pause before Gabriel settled back upon the pillows with a wry smile.

"Well, I should not wish our rose garden to be askew. Will you return and share lunch with me?"

Beatrice's first instinct was to refuse. She had always avoided Gabriel's presence, perhaps sensing she would never be proof against his potent charm.

Then, meeting the steady hazel gaze, she discovered herself giving a slow nod of her head.

It would hardly be proper to abandon him when he was wounded and confined to his bed, she swiftly reassured herself.

It was her duty to be at his side.

"If you wish."

"I wish it very much." His smile widened, a teasing glint returning to his eye. "Do not bully the workers too fiercely, my dear."

She placed her hands upon her hips. "I never bully the workmen."

He gave a sudden laugh. "You are an outrageous bully, but Falcon Park will be a spectacular success for your efforts. Our children will someday thank you."

Our children.

A dangerous warmth threatened to fill her heart.

Gabriel's children.

"I shall return later," she muttered, and fled the room with considerably more haste than elegance.

Gabriel watched his wife's awkward retreat with a combination of amusement and regret.

He did not believe he would ever tire of her flustered confusion whenever he touched her or whispered words of desire.

On the other hand, he was becoming desperately weary of longing for a woman who refused to belong fully to him.

His body ached with frustration. A frustration made only worse by the knowledge that he could stir Beatrice's passions if she would but put the past behind them.

Before his marriage, he might have made a trip to the local village to discover a willing barmaid. Or even sought the company of the lovely Widow Alton, who had been more than forward in her attentions.

Now, however, the mere thought made him shudder.

He had made a commitment when he married Beatrice. He promised her fidelity when he placed his ring upon her finger. He would not deceive her yet again.

And in truth, he had no desire for a swift, meaningless coupling. He wanted his wife. The woman he could hold in his arms throughout the night. The woman who would someday bear his children.

He drew in a deep breath, willing his stiff body to relax.

It appeared he was in the damnable position of desiring the only woman he could not have.

Damnable, indeed.

Heaving a sigh, Gabriel reached up to lightly finger the plaster upon his forehead. And now to add to his ill luck, he was commanded to his bed by a demented doctor who was clearly determined to torture him beyond all bearing.

"Well, my lord, that was quite a scare you gave us."

Gabriel turned toward the vicar, standing in the door. He smiled at the welcome interruption to his brooding thoughts.

"Ah, Humbly, come in."

The man waddled happily forward, his hair sticking out in a dozen different directions.

"How are you feeling?"

"Like every sort of a fool," Gabriel admitted with a grimace. "I did warn you that I was hopeless at such nonsense. Instead of winning my lady's favor, I very nearly got us both killed."

Taking a chair beside the bed, the vicar smiled with a hint of complacency.

"Perhaps it did not all turn out according to your plan, but I assure you that Beatrice was most distressed when she arrived at the house. She was genuinely concerned for your welfare."

The reminder of precisely how Beatrice had returned to the house sent a fresh flare of anger through Gabriel.

The very thought that she had so recklessly risked her life made him wish to slam his fist into something very hard.

"She should have been throttled," he muttered.

The older gentleman lifted his brows in surprise. "Pardon me?"

"She took a boat onto a storm-tossed lake that even I would hesitate to attempt without the barest ability to swim. One errant wave and she would now be—" He gave a deep shudder. "Gads, I cannot even bear to think of it."

Astonishingly, the vicar merely shrugged. "Beatrice is a woman of tremendous courage and resourcefulness. You surely did not suppose she would be content to weakly await rescue after you had been injured?"

Well, of course he knew his wife was a woman of courage and resourcefulness, for goodness' sake. She was also far more intelligent than any other person he had ever encountered. Unfortunately, she had failed to use her God-given wits when she had climbed into that boat.

"I thought she possessed more sense than to so absurdly risk her life," he growled.

"She was quite desperate."

"She had no right to expose herself to such danger, no matter how desperate she was."

A vaguely disturbing smile touched the round countenance. "Yes, well, it is done and all is well," he soothed.

Gabriel forced himself to thrust aside the horrid image of Beatrice upon the raging lake. He had no doubt it would haunt him for years.

"I suppose."

"And you cannot deny the incident revealed that Beatrice is still very attached to you."

"Perhaps," he slowly agreed.

"It is a very good omen."

Gabriel was not nearly so optimistic.

"But she no longer trusts me. And without trust our marriage is doomed."

"You must have patience, my son."

Patience? Gabriel ground his teeth. He was beginning to detest that word.

"Easy enough for you to say."

Humbly chuckled. "Yes, I suppose it is."

Rather sheepishly realizing he was being deliberately contrary, Gabriel summoned a lopsided grin.

"Forgive me. I am told that I am a very petulant invalid."

A twinkle entered the sherry eyes. "Yes, I did hear as much from the good doctor."

"Gads, the man was fortunate that I was too weak to have him tossed out on his ear. Do you know that wretched fool poked me from head to toe and then threatened to have me bled when I complained?"

"No one enjoys the attentions of a doctor, especially when it means being confined to bed."

"I shall no doubt go mad," Gabriel readily agreed. "Why do I not find a chessboard and we can have a game or two?"

Despite his reluctance to be left to his own devices, Gabriel knew he should protest. The poor gentleman had not come all the way to Derbyshire to entertain an invalid.

"Surely you would prefer to be exploring the countryside or visiting your friend?"

"Not at all," the vicar stoutly denied. "There is nothing I enjoy more than a rousing game of chess."

"Well, I cannot promise a rousing game," Gabriel warned. "It has been years since I have attempted my skill at chess, but I would appreciate the company."

Humbly promptly rose to his feet. "Good. I shall return in a few moments with the board."

The vicar left the room with a decided spring in his step.

Things were coming along quite nicely, he decided with a knowing smile.

Perhaps Gabriel and Beatrice had not yet fully comprehended the depths of their true feelings for each other, but they had made decided progress.

Beatrice had willingly risked her life to save her husband. And Gabriel had suddenly been forced to think of a world without Beatrice.

Both had been badly shaken by the incident. And both were now forced to genuinely confront the emotions that had been so unexpectedly exposed.

With a bit more prodding, he would surely have the two of them happily settled.

Busily congratulating his fine work, Humbly made his way toward the distant kitchens. He would ask Cook where to find the chessboard, he told himself, and at the same time perhaps discover a tasty snack to tide him until luncheon.

A lovely lemon tart would certainly still the grumbling in his stomach. Or perhaps a scone fresh from the oven.

Lost in his thoughts of delicate pastries, Humbly had no sense of impending doom. In fact, it was not until a shrill voice split the peaceful silence that he realized his danger.

"Mr. Humbly."

Muttering a less than devout curse, Humbly came to a halt and watched Mrs. Quarry hurry in his direction.

"Oh, Mr. Humbly," she cried. "At last I have found you."

He gave a stiff bow. "Mrs. Quarry."

"Naughty man." She waved a bony finger directly in his face. "Have you been hiding from me?"

Rather childishly, Humbly stuck his hands behind his back and crossed his fingers.

"Of course not."

"But I have not seen you about at all," she complained.

Humbly knew he should feel a measure of guilt at having so assiduously avoided the widow. But he had not managed to remain a content bachelor for nearly sixty years by being a ready target for desperate females. A gentleman had to be swift upon his feet to avoid the numerous traps they could lay.

"Yes, well, I have been rather busy visiting my friend and, of course, becoming better acquainted with Lord Faulconer."

"I see." Astonishingly, the thin lips managed a well-rehearsed quiver. "I suppose it was too much to hope you would have time for a foolish old widow."

Humbly nervously cleared his throat. "I . . . that is . . ."

"No, no. I understand." The woman magically produced a handkerchief to dab at her thin nose. "You mustn't change your schedule to worry over me. I assure you I am quite accustomed to being ignored. It is the lot of the poor relative, you know. And I would never presume to push myself where I was not wanted."

Despite the realization that the woman was blatantly attempting to stir his pity, Humbly found himself weakening.

Whatever her annoying tendencies, she was still one of God's creatures, he reminded himself reluctantly. It was his duty to provide what comfort he could.

"Perhaps we could share tea later this afternoon," he grudgingly offered.

She patted her nose again. "Well, I shouldn't wish to be a bother."

"It is no bother."

"You are quite certain?"

He swallowed a sigh. "Quite certain."

Within the blink of an eye the downtrodden martyr had been replaced by a smugly confident female. The handkerchief disappeared and a predatory glint entered the pale eyes.

"Then, I must meet with Cook," she chattered as she tapped her finger to her narrow chin. "Do not think I haven't noticed how well you enjoy those lovely lemon tarts. And, of course, plenty of cucumber sandwiches."

Humbly shuddered. Mrs. Quarry and cucumber sandwiches? Dear heavens, what had he done to deserve such a wretched fate?

"Cucumber sandwiches?" he said weakly.

The widow smiled coyly. "A gentleman of your age must think of his health."

"You are not related to Mrs. Stalwart, are you?"

She batted her stubby lashes in confusion. "Mrs. Stalwart? No, I do not believe so. Is she an acquaintance of yours?"

"Never mind." He performed a resigned bow. "I shall see you later."

"Do not forget me," she warned.

"I do not believe it is even a possibility," he muttered.

She gave a shrill giggle. "Oh, Vicar, what a tease you are."

Turning on his heel, Humbly made his way back to Gabriel's chambers. He would have one of the endless footmen go in search of the deuced chessboard.

And on the next occasion he would not allow the rumblings of his stomach to put him off his guard, he told himself.

The temptation of lemon tarts was not worth the torture of an afternoon in the company of Mrs. Quarry.

Not unless there also happened to be one of those nice muffins or a tasty sponge cake.

Eleven

After two days of being kept a virtual prisoner in his bed, Gabriel expected to be a ready candidate for Bedlam.

He was, after all, a gentleman accustomed to endless activity. Work about the estate kept him on the run from the moment he awoke until he tumbled into his bed late in the evening. If he wasn't in the fields or meeting with his steward, then he was in his study, attempting to sort through years of neglected ledger books.

To suddenly be trapped in his chamber with nothing to occupy him but the occasional visitor was surely worse than being placed upon the rack.

But much to his surprise, he found an unexpected benefit to being an invalid.

Covertly turning his head, Gabriel regarded his wife, who was seated close to his bed as she fiercely studied a handful of fabric swatches.

Each day Beatrice had spent a portion of her time seated close beside him. Whether reading to him from the morning paper or simply sharing what progress had been made by the workmen, she had revealed a bit more about herself.

He now knew that she was well read on the latest politics and held very firm views on the plight of children and the troubles faced by soldiers returning home from the war with no jobs and few opportunities. He also discovered that she closely followed the 'Change and knew precisely the worth of the stocks that were held by her father. Perhaps more surprisingly he learned she possessed a lighthearted interest in the current gossip that filled the scandal sheets.

The charming insights into her character only made her more precious to Gabriel.

Somehow he had always suspected that a large dose of familiarity would lead to a disgust for each other. Certainly a number of his married friends had warned him of just such a disaster. But as he was allowed to glimpse deeper into Beatrice's thoughts and feelings, he found himself eager to discover more.

She was a fascinating mixture of practical common sense and soft-hearted liberalism. She could be fiery in defense of the helpless and impishly amusing when recalling stories of her days among the *ton*.

She was also deeply lonely.

As lonely as himself.

The knowledge made him more determined than ever to reach out and forge a bond between them.

They clearly needed each other.

If only he could prove to her that he was worthy of her trust.

Easier said than done, he acknowledged with an inward sigh.

His gaze ran a restless path over the pale features that had become so endearingly familiar. Then a faint smile tugged at his lips as he noted how she frowned over the bits of fabric.

"So serious, my dear?" he softly broke into her dark thoughts.

Lifting her head, she held out the samples for his inspection.

"I cannot determine which color most closely resembles the draperies in the library. What is your opinion?"

Gabriel glanced over the offered fabrics with a lift of his brows.

"Good gads, they all look the same."

"Of course they do not," she protested. "This is a much darker shade, while this one possesses a hint of plum."

He laughed as he shook his head. "I shall have to take your word for it."

She heaved a sigh as she fingered a threadbare square of fabric. "I do wish the original were not so faded. It is impossible to determine the precise color."

Gabriel settled himself more comfortably in the pillows, as always amazed by Beatrice's obvious devotion to Falcon Park.

"Surely the color of the draperies in the library is not of such prime importance?"

"I should like it to be as close as possible."

"You have truly taken on a tremendous task, my dear," he said in genuine admiration.

As always, she turned a flustered pink at his words of praise. He had already determined that she was unaccustomed to having her talents admired.

"I do not mind."

"Still, it is very generous of you," he persisted.

"This is my home as well as yours now."

His heart warmed at her words. Falcon Park was indeed becoming a home again. And it was all due to this woman's inexhaustible efforts.

"Yes, but most brides would prefer to redecorate in a more modern style," he retorted with a rueful smile. "It would be far simpler than devoting such energy to restoring the house to its previous glory."

She shrugged aside the vast burden she had so willingly shouldered.

"I hope it will be worth the effort."

Gabriel reached out to gently cover her hand with his own. "Have I thanked you yet for all you've done for Falcon Park?"

Amazingly, she managed to blush a deeper shade of red. "There is no need," she mumbled. "I am your wife."

"My wife." He savored the words as if they were a fine wine. "I very much like the sound of that."

He felt her sudden tremor even as she battled to maintain an air of cool control.

"You are being absurd."

"No, I am not." He captured her gaze with his own. "As I said, I never thought I would have a family. I am finding that I enjoy being a part of one with you. It is very comforting to know you will be here when I awaken in the morning, to think of you strolling in the garden, or to catch the scent of honeysuckle when I enter the room. It gives me a sense of belonging here that I have not felt since my mother died."

The amber eyes abruptly darkened. "Oh."

Gabriel glanced down to where his larger hand covered her fingers. "I only wish that you felt more comfortable here."

"I—it has only been a few months since I arrived. And with the workmen—"

"Perhaps I should say that I wish you felt more comfortable with me," he softly interrupted her stumbling words. "Do you recall the first evening we met?"

There was a faint pause before she gave a nod of her head. "Of course."

"I had been introduced to what seemed like a hundred maidens since arriving in London, but the moment

I was in your company, I realized that you were the only woman who I felt as if I had known my entire life."

She regarded him with obvious disbelief. "I find that difficult to believe. I was so nervous, I chattered like the veriest nitwit."

Gabriel gave a low chuckle as he recalled their brief encounter. At the time he had known nothing about her beyond the fact that she possessed a large fortune and was reputed to be decidedly eccentric.

He had prepared himself for yet another shallow miss who had been sternly tutored in the proper behavior for a debutant. No matter what the rumors of Beatrice's odd manners, he refused to hope she would dare to be anything but tediously proper.

It had been a refreshing treat when she had boldly spoken her mind without apology and without artifice. He had been instantly intrigued by the unconventional maiden.

"You were charming," he said in firm tones, a reminiscent smile playing about his mouth. "And you certainly did not chatter."

"Yes, I did," she perversely argued. "I told you of my dislike of London, of my grandfather, of my inventions. I think I even told you that my shoes were pinching my toes."

He shrugged, his fingers unconsciously stroking the back of her hand and delicate curve of her wrist.

"That was far preferable to the stiff conversations of the weather or latest fashions I endured. There were even some maidens who managed no more than a number of nerve-shattering giggles. You cannot conceive my relief to discover a woman who could share a sensible conversation. I even recall that you wore a pale green gown with satin ivory roses."

She abruptly ducked her head, although she did not attempt to pull free from his light caress.

"I fear that was my mother's notion of a suitable gown for a debutant. I attempted to warn her that I looked unfortunately like an underripe apple, but she would not heed my warnings."

With an impatient click of his tongue, Gabriel reached up to cup her chin and forced her to meet his narrowed gaze.

"Why do you say such things of yourself?" he demanded.

She appeared startled by his disapproving tone. "It is habit, I suppose."

"I will not have it in my presence," he informed her sternly. "The only one who finds you wanting in any fashion is yourself."

There was a stark silence before he heard her heave a faint sigh.

"It is not always comfortable to be considered different by others."

Gabriel was not to be swayed. Certainly he could sympathize with desiring the approval of others. He had lived through a similar battle with his own father. But he would not allow her to belittle her worth.

"Surely your grandfather did not apologize for being different?"

She gave a reluctant smile. "Goodness, no. He did not give a fig for others' opinions."

"A wise man. You should follow his example. You are Beatrice, Countess of Faulconer. Hold your head proudly and know that those who truly care about you desire you to remain precisely as you are."

Their gazes locked for a long while as Gabriel silently willed his stubborn wife to realize just how wonderful she truly was.

"I shall try," she at last conceded. "Now I must go. You need your rest."

Gabriel grasped her fingers, which had thankfully healed over the past two days. He had no desire to have their time together come to an end.

"Gads, all I have done is rest. I am bored senseless."

"I know that the vicar spent the entire morning playing chess with you," she chided with a teasing frown. "Not to mention the fact that the servants have transferred the entire contents of the library to your chamber as well as newspapers and your estate ledgers. How could you possibly be bored?"

He wrinkled his nose in distaste. "I do not wish to read."

"Would you prefer that I send Aunt Sarah to bear you company?"

He greeted her sweet words with a jaundiced frown. "I suppose you are attempting to be humorous? I would as soon desire the return of that devilish doctor to gouge me."

"I could send the carriage to fetch him."

He abruptly lifted her hand to press it to his lips. "What I want is for you to remain."

She trembled at his touch, but with an annoying determination she rose to her feet and pulled her hand free.

"I cannot."

"Cannot or will not?"

"Gabriel."

He sighed at the stubborn line of her jaw. He knew that expression all too well.

"You will at least return later?"

"Yes." With an uncertain smile she gathered her samples of fabric and hurried from the room.

Left on his own, Gabriel shook his head slowly.

He felt so close to reaching Beatrice. As if any moment she would smile and welcome him back into her heart.

And then, without warning, she would retreat behind her wary distrust.

Would he ever have the wife he so desperately desired?

Although Beatrice had fled from Gabriel's chambers with every intention of devoting the afternoon to the various tenants she had been sadly neglecting, she discovered herself instead standing at the window of her office.

It was not that she was particularly fascinated by Chalfrey's shrill protests as the workmen laid the new paths for the rose garden, or even the glorious sunset that bathed the countryside in a rosy hue.

Instead, she pondered the strange and complex emotions that battled within her heart.

How was a mere woman to know what she was feeling?

On one hand, she had been forced to concede that she still cared for Gabriel. The pain and desperation she had experienced when he had been injured could not be denied. And too, over the past two days they had shared moments that were as wonderful and precious as the days of their brief courtship. And yet he was still the same gentleman who had deliberately wed her for her fortune.

Could she simply forgive and forget what he had done?

Did she want to?

It was that question that kept her standing at the window long after the workmen had retired from their duties and dinner had been served.

She hoped that by searching her heart she would

eventually discover the truth that had evaded her for so long.

"So deep in thought, Beatrice?"

Startled by the sudden interruption, Beatrice turned about to regard Vicar Humbly as he strolled into the room. She experienced a pang of guilt as she realized that she had condemned the poor gentleman to the mercy of Aunt Sarah. Hardly sporting of her.

"Mr. Humbly." She managed a distracted smile. "I did not hear you enter."

He tilted his head to one side. "No, you were glaring fiercely out the window. What dark thoughts have brought such a scowl to your pretty countenance?"

Disconcerted by the older man's piercing scrutiny, Beatrice shifted uneasily.

"No dark thoughts at all. I was simply contemplating one of the inventions I recently viewed."

"Oh? Which invention?" he swiftly demanded.

"What?"

"I asked which invention."

"I . . ."

His lips twitched as she struggled to invent a suitable lie. "You were thinking of Gabriel, were you not?"

Realizing that she had been easily outwitted, Beatrice heaved a sigh.

"Yes."

Humbly moved close enough to grasp her hands in his own. "Has his condition worsened?"

"No," Beatrice was swift to reassure him. "The doctor says that he may leave his bed tomorrow."

"But surely that is wonderful news?"

"Oh, yes, quite wonderful."

The vicar studied her tense features. "So why do you frown?"

Unable to dissemble beneath that steady gaze, she gave a sad smile.

"Marriage is a very complicated business."

He gave her hands a soft squeeze. "All relationships are complicated, my dear. Please, will you sit with me a moment?"

"Very well," she agreed, allowing herself to be led to the small sofa set beside the carved marble chimney-piece.

Waiting until they were both settled upon the crimson damask sofa, Humbly offered her a kindly smile.

"Do you know, when I was merely a young lad I used to love to go fishing."

Beatrice gave a startled blink at his odd words. "I suppose all boys love to go fishing."

"Yes." A reminiscent expression settled upon his round countenance. "There was a small river quite near our house, and during the afternoon I would spend hours frightening the fish away. Unfortunately, I also ended every afternoon at the bottom of the river."

Presuming the tenderhearted gentleman was attempting to distract her troubled thoughts, Beatrice forced a stiff smile to her lips.

"You were so clumsy?"

"No. The neighborhood children thought me rather a source for jest and enjoyed tumbling me into the water."

Beatrice gave a soft gasp. It was unthinkable that anyone could be so cruel to this sweet man.

"That is terrible."

The older gentleman grimaced. "I certainly thought so at the time. I began searching for hidden places along the river where I would not be discovered by the others. I became very good at it."

"They were horrid boys," she said fiercely, all too

aware of how deeply the taunts of children could hurt. She was fortunate to have had Addy and Victoria, who had always stood at her side.

"No more than most young boys," Humbly retorted with a shrug. "They were only attempting to show off for one another."

"Well, at least you were able to fish in peace," she said, wondering if she could be so forgiving.

"Yes, I even had a friend who would join me now and then. Georgie Dicart. He was the youngest son of the local doctor and often at the mercy of the older boys as well."

"So the two of you stuck together?"

There was a short pause before Humbly heaved a sigh. "We did until the day he led the other boys to my hidden place. You see, he hoped to impress them by offering me as his sacrifice."

Beatrice instinctively reached out to grasp his hand. Her heart was deeply touched by the betrayal he must have experienced.

"Oh, no."

"I was devastated, of course," he admitted with a hint of sadness in his sherry eyes. "Not so much for being tossed in the water once again—after all, I was quite accustomed to dragging myself home soaked to the skin—but because my friend, the one person I trusted, had betrayed me."

Beatrice slowly stiffened as she sensed that the vicar was not simply attempting to distract her with his childhood tale. He clearly intended to reveal that she was not the only one to have offered her trust and had it destroyed.

"Yes," she said slowly.

"I cried at first," he continued in low tones, "then, like most twelve-year-old boys, I began plotting my revenge.

I wanted him to feel as embarrassed and hurt as I had been."

Even knowing that Humbly had a devious intent behind his story, Beatrice could not resist discovering where the wily old man was attempting to lead her.

"What did you do?"

"I waited until we had all gathered in church on Sunday, then in the middle of the sermon I stood and accused Georgie of stealing from the poor box."

Beatrice widened her eyes in shock. "Good heavens."

"It was quite effective." The vicar gave a rueful shake of his head. "The congregation fell silent and the boy's father yanked him to his feet and beat him in the presence of the entire neighborhood. I shall never forget the look upon my friend's face."

Beatrice was startled in spite of herself. It was impossible to imagine this kind, generous man ever harming anyone.

"I suppose he looked as if he hated you?" she asked gently.

Humbly gave a shake of his head. "No. The look upon his countenance was one of relief. He had felt so guilty at having deceived me that he was eager to be punished. I left the church feeling like the most loathsome creature on earth."

Beatrice's heart squeezed with a sudden flare of pain.

There was no means to avoid the obvious connection to her and Gabriel.

Like Humbly, she had been betrayed and struck out in fury. While Gabriel had reacted just as Georgie with his readiness to accept her punishment as his just reward.

And in the end, she did feel like the most loathsome creature on earth.

She bit her bottom lip as she met his steady gaze. "You no doubt are referring to me and Gabriel."

"I merely wish you to look into your heart, Beatrice," he said softly. "Is punishing Gabriel making you happy?"

She gave a restless shake of her head, wishing it were all so simple.

"It is not just a matter of punishment, it is a matter of trust. Did you ever again tell Georgie where you went to go fishing?"

Humbly smiled complacently. "Of course I did. He was my friend. He made a mistake, but then again, so did I. Friends forgive one another."

Her eyes darkened with the fear that had haunted her since her wedding day.

"And what if he betrays me again?"

His expression became unexpectedly stern. "My dear, none of us can see into the future. But surely he has proven over the past few months that he wants your happiness above all things?"

"I suppose," she agreed warily.

"It is not wise to brood upon past wounds. In time they will poison your soul. You must look to the future now. Decide if you wish it to be filled with this brittle anger or if you would be better served to find peace with your husband."

Beatrice gave a slow nod of her head. "I will consider your words."

"That is all that I ask." He reached out to lightly pat her cheek. "Good night, my dear."

"Good night."

The vicar struggled to his feet and slowly left Beatrice alone with her thoughts.

For many moments she pondered the vicar's words, knowing he was only saying out loud what she had realized deep in her heart.

Gabriel was her husband.

She had promised to be at his side for the rest of her life.

Did she wish to continue this empty battle that made both of them miserable?

Or did she risk her heart once again and seek the happiness she had once hoped was hers?

Barely aware that she was moving, Beatrice rose to her feet and walked toward the door.

It was time she confronted her fears.

And the only way to do so was with the help of Gabriel.

Twelve

Gabriel set aside the large tray of food he had left largely untasted. His usually ravenous appetite had been stolen not only by the hours of simply lying in bed, but also by the long afternoon awaiting Beatrice's return.

Where the devil was she?

He knew from the servants that she had not left the house. Nor was she with the workmen or visiting with Mr. Humbly. He had also discovered she had not made an appearance for dinner.

Clearly, something was troubling her, he decided. Beatrice always retreated within herself when she had something upon her mind.

But what?

With stubborn tenacity his mind had gone over their brief encounter earlier in the day. Could he have said or done something to annoy her? Had she perhaps been frightened by his harmless kiss upon her hand?

At last he conceded defeat.

How the deuce was a mere man ever to understand the mysterious workings of the female mind? He might as well contemplate the ancient philosophies or distant stars. He had as much a chance of deciphering their meaning as understanding his wife.

This dark knowledge had instilled a restless ache within him.

He longed to leave his bed and seek Beatrice out. He wanted to confront her and demand to know why she had so rudely deserted him. He wanted to shake her until she admitted she still cared for him. He wanted to pull her into his arms and drown in her pleasure.

Instead, he could only lie in his bed and curse the moment he had decided to wed Beatrice without confessing his need for her fortune.

What a fool he had been. He had traded in his hopes for love to save a moldering pile of stone and tenants who would never understand the sacrifices he had made for them.

What a damnable, damnable mess.

He was so intent upon his self-recriminations that he barely noted the door to his chamber being pushed slowly open. Then his heart gave a sudden leap as Beatrice cautiously entered.

"Beatrice," he breathed, his gaze anxiously surveying her pale features.

"Am I intruding?"

"Of course not." He waited until she had hesitantly crossed the room to perch upon the chair that he kept situated close to his bed. "You are pale, my dear. Is something the matter?"

"I . . . I think that we should speak of our marriage," she confessed in low tones.

It was what he had desired to do from the moment she had discovered the truth behind their hasty marriage. All he had wanted was the opportunity to convince her that he had never meant to hurt her. That he had always intended to be a good and faithful husband.

Now, however, he discovered himself decidedly wary.

What if she had decided that she wished to leave Falcon Park?

Perhaps she had even determined to seek a divorce.

Could he let her go?

Could he bear to give her up if that was what would give her happiness?

Unconsciously he squared his shoulders.

Yes.

As much as it might rip at his heart. As much as it might condemn him to a life of barren loneliness, he would allow her to leave if that was what she truly wished.

How could he not give her the opportunity to seek the happiness he had denied her?

She deserved so much better than a life filled with bitter regret.

It was all very noble.

So why the devil did he feel as if the life were being ruthlessly squeezed from his very soul?

"Very well, my dear," he at last forced the words past his stiff lips.

"I . . ." She stumbled to a halt, appearing as reluctant as himself to begin the discussion.

"Yes, Beatrice?"

She gazed down at the hands she had clenched in her lap. "This is not easy."

Gabriel gritted his teeth. "You are not thinking of leaving Falcon Park, are you?"

Her head abruptly lifted. "No."

"Good." He slowly released the breath he had not even realized he was holding. She wasn't leaving. He still had a chance. "As much as I desire you to be happy, I should be lost without you here. You have become an essential part of my life."

"Hardly essential," she protested in breathy tones.

"Utterly essential," he countered, determinedly holding her gaze with his own. "You are the one person who loves Falcon Park and the people who depend upon us as much as I. More than that, you are my wife. My true partner."

"I have not been a very good wife," she said ruefully.

"You had little cause to take pride in the position."

Her gaze once again returned to her hands. "When I discovered that you were in need of a fortune, I was very hurt."

Gabriel briefly closed his eyes against the wave of sharp regret.

"I am sorry, my dear."

"I felt as if I had been betrayed by the one person I had come to trust."

"Yes," he breathed softly.

"And I suppose I wished to punish you for having deceived me."

His lips twisted. Her cold distaste had been punishment indeed. He would as soon face a firing squad.

"You have been very efficient," he said dryly.

Surprisingly, Beatrice gave a faint wince. "But not very happy."

"No," he agreed.

"Vicar Humbly warns me that I must not cling to my anger. That it will poison my soul."

Gabriel sent a silent prayer of thanks toward the bumbling old gentleman. Obviously the vicar had been doing his share to ease Beatrice's troubled doubt.

"He is a very wise man."

"Yes, but . . ."

"What?"

She slowly lifted her head, the amber eyes dark with uncertainty. "I do not know how."

Gabriel resisted the urge to pull her into his arms and demonstrate just how easy it could be to put the past behind them. He might be able to make her body respond to his touch, but he needed more. He wanted her heart.

"Do you know, Beatrice, when I first joined my regiment that I always forced my way to the midst of the fighting?" he said gently, forcing himself to thrust aside his dislike of recalling the heedless, uncertain youth he had been when he had fled from Falcon Park. "I was a reckless fool who courted death all because my father had always considered me a weak coward. I was determined to prove him wrong even if it meant my own death."

She paled to a near white as she regarded him with a satisfying expression of horror.

"Gabriel."

He gave a rueful lift of one shoulder. "It was my colonel who took me aside and sternly informed me that it took less courage to die than to live and face the troubles each of us have in our life. He was right, of course. It did take more courage to live. Especially after I returned home to discover the disaster my father had made of the estate. And then, when you turned from me and I realized how badly I had hurt you. There was more than one morning when I desired to simply walk away and leave it all behind."

She regarded him for a moment before giving a slow nod of her head.

"Yes."

He carefully considered his words, not wishing to press her too forcibly. The mere fact that she was willing to discuss her hurt and disappointment was a good omen. He could not risk rushing her.

"Just as for you it would be easier to continue hating me than to risk forgiving me and being hurt again."

A measure of surprise rippled over her pale features. "I have never hated you."

He arched a brow. "No?"

"Of course not."

"Oh, I think you did. If only just a little."

"Really, Gabriel," she protested.

With a low laugh he reached out to collect one of her tightly clenched fists.

"I do dare to hope, however, that such a rousing dislike has faded over time."

"I never hated or even disliked you, Gabriel," she insisted, unconsciously leaning forward. "I simply lost my faith in you."

Although prepared for honesty, Gabriel discovered his breath catching at the knife-edged pain that plunged into his heart.

"Beatrice, I cannot promise never to disappoint you again. No one can make such a promise," he said in husky tones. "But I do swear upon all that is holy that I will never purposely deceive you. I have learned a very bitter lesson."

She was silent for a long while before giving a tilt of her chin.

"And I will try to be a better wife."

"No." He gave her fingers a warning squeeze. "I want you to be happy. That is what I want in my wife."

"I will try."

He couldn't help but chuckle at her obedient tone. "You sound like a child trying to please an adult."

An enchanting color touched her cheeks. "All I mean is that it will take time."

"I am a very patient man," he soothed, conveniently forgetting his increasing bursts of impatience that had plagued him for the past fortnight.

"Yes, I have noticed that about you," she agreed.

His smile twisted. "Although I will admit that my patience is being sorely tested at the moment. To have my wife in my bed is a pleasure that I have longed for far too long."

He felt the fingers wrapped in his own tremble at his low words.

"Oh."

"Does it bother you for me to speak of my desire for you?" he demanded.

Her gaze lowered with a charming hint of confusion. "It does seem strange to discuss such things."

"There are more pleasurable means of revealing my desires," he softly prompted, his hand trailing up her arm in a provocative caress. "This bed is quite wide enough for both of us and far more comfortable than that chair."

Her head jerked upward at his determined proposition. "But you are injured."

"A trifling scratch. I assure you that it does not bother me a wit."

"The doctor said that you should not excite yourself."

Gabriel wryly acknowledged that it was far too late for such a warning. If having his heart racing with anticipation and his body stirring with need was going to cause his sudden demise, then they should be digging his grave.

"That doctor is a fussy old fool," he said firmly, gazing deep into her eyes. "Beatrice, may I hold you?"

She was silent for so long that Gabriel was already preparing himself for yet another rejection. Gads, he should be accustomed to being treated as if he carried the plague, he grimly told himself. Beatrice had made it painfully clear that she did not yet trust him. He had been a nodcock to press her.

Then his breath was wrenched from his body as she gave a slow nod of her head.

"Very well."

With endearingly awkward motions she rose from the chair and climbed onto the bed. Gabriel barely dared to move as she battled her skirts and settled beside him. He did not wish to do anything that might frighten her into sudden flight. But when she nearly knocked them both senseless by ramming her head into his chin, he decided it was time to take charge of the astonishing situation.

With a low laugh he gently pushed her down against the mattress and rolled onto his side so he could openly regard her nervous countenance.

"Relax, Beatrice," he coaxed, his hand lifting of its own accord to lightly trace a path over the tempting silk of her cheek. "I promise I will not do anything that does not please you." He patiently waited for the tension to drain from her body, his fingers continuing to stroke her face. "Your skin fascinates me. It is so soft, so perfectly smooth." He shifted to swiftly remove the pins from her hair, spreading the curls across the white pillow. "And this hair. The color of honey."

Her lips slightly parted. "Does it please you?"

A shudder raced through his body.

Please him?

Lucifer's teeth.

If he were any more pleased, he could not possibly bear the exquisite agony.

"Everything about you pleases me. Those magnificent eyes, the curve of your lips, the very delightful—"

"Gabriel." She gave a choked laugh as his gaze moved down to her disheveled neckline.

"Yes, my dearest?" he murmured.

The amber eyes slowly darkened. "Kiss me."

His heart stumbled to a halt.

Then slowly, almost nervously, he lowered his head.

"Whatever my lady desires," he promised softly.

* * *

Gabriel leaned upon his elbow as he studied his sleeping wife.

Wife.

He slowly smiled.

She was indeed his wife. In every sense of the word.

How lovely she had been last evening.

As sweet and giving as he had always sensed she would be. And while her responses had been shyly innocent, she had provided him with a pleasure that he could only marvel upon.

He gently reached out to stroke a honey curl from her cheek. Yes, she had certainly given him pleasure, he acknowledged with a flare of tenderness, but what they had shared went far beyond mere physical release.

Each touch, each kiss, had only deepened the unexplainable bond that had been forged between them.

This was his woman, he had realized in the most secret center of his heart. His true mate that completed him in a manner that filled him with awe.

The knowledge made him long to climb atop the roof and shout for joy. Surely no one had ever been as happy and content as he felt at this moment?

Perhaps sensing his intense regard, Beatrice slowly stirred. Then the thick lashes lifted and he was staring into the bemused amber eyes.

For a moment Gabriel tensed, terrified that she might regret their night of passion. Gads, he couldn't bear to think of her bringing shame to such a glorious experience. But even as he held his breath in dread, a tentative smile touched her lips.

"Good morning," she said in husky tones.

His breath rushed out in profound relief. Her cheeks

were flushed, but a lingering pleasure darkened those eyes.

"Good morning, my dear." His fingers moved to trace the line of her jaw. "How do you feel?"

"Quite well, thank you."

He smiled as her blush deepened. "I am feeling glorious this morning. It is very nice to sleep with my wife in bed beside me."

Her lashes fluttered downward. "It is rather different to share a bed, is it not?"

"It certainly is." He deliberately shifted until his body was pressed intimately next to her own. His heart quickened as he felt her tremble in anticipation. "The warmth of another body quite made up for the snoring and kicking. I did not even mind that you stole all the covers."

Her gaze flew upward in mock outrage. "Snoring? I do not snore, and I certainly do not kick. And you, sir, are the one who steals covers."

Pleased that his teasing had melted her lingering embarrassment, Gabriel trailed his fingers down the curve of her neck. He discovered awakening with his wife in his arms was a delicious treat. A treat he intended to take full advantage of.

"A despicable lie," he retorted. "A gentleman never steals the covers."

She wrinkled her nose at him. "Well, a lady does not snore."

"Perhaps I was mistaken," he admitted, becoming increasingly distracted as his fingers explored her satin skin.

She shivered. "Yes."

"Mmm . . ." He watched in fascination as the amber eyes dilated with a rising passion. "I do not suppose I could convince you to remain here for a while?"

"How long a while?"

His caresses became even more determined as his body stirred with a growing need.

"Oh . . . a month?"

She gave a choked laugh. "Really, Gabriel."

"A week, then?" he graciously compromised.

She shook her head even as her body arched beneath his demanding touch.

"Certainly not."

He lowered his head to place a kiss upon her brow. "You are a harsh woman."

"No, merely a busy one," she breathed, giving a choked moan as his arm encircled her waist and tugged her firmly against his hard body. "Just think of all the workmen awaiting my orders, and the merchants who seek my patronage and the tenants and servants . . . oh."

He skillfully teased the corner of her mouth. "You do not mean to imply that the choosing of fabrics or viewing of inventions holds more appeal than remaining here, do you?"

Her own hands tentatively rose to explore the muscles of his chest. Gabriel shuddered in delicious response.

"Well, there is nothing quite so exciting as a well-made machine," she informed him.

Gabriel growled deep in his throat. "You desire excitement, do you, wench? Well, I can give you all the excitement you desire."

Her eyes widened as he rolled atop her.

"Gabriel."

He gave a low chuckle, feeling as if his entire body were on fire. Dear heavens, it could not be natural for a man to desire his wife with such a force. If it were, no husband on earth would ever have a mistress.

"I do like this sharing of a bed," he murmured, his fingers threading into the honey curls.

She offered him a mysterious smile of contentment.

"Even if I snore?"

"You have a delightful snore, my dear," he assured her, his lips moving to worship her pale features. "And a delightful brow, and nose and chin . . ."

"Gabriel," she whispered huskily.

"Yes, my dear?"

"Kiss me."

His blood rushed with molten heat. "Anything you desire."

With exquisite care Gabriel covered her lips with his own, tasting deeply of her sweetness. His kiss became more demanding as her arms reached up to tangle in his hair. At that moment he was quite certain a month in bed with his wife was not nearly long enough.

Intent on coaxing Beatrice's ready desire, Gabriel did not note the knock upon the door. It was not until the unwelcome voice of his valet floated through the thick wood that he realized the world outside was about to intrude.

"Pardon me, my lord."

Gritting his teeth in annoyance, Gabriel lifted his head. "Go away, Saunders."

"But, my lord, the workers insist upon speaking with Lady Faulconer," the servant retorted.

Gabriel briefly considered sacking the whole lot of them. How the devil would he ever have Beatrice to himself when a hundred servants, artists, architects, and workmen were constantly demanding her attention? Then sanity reluctantly returned. He supposed it was rather unrealistic to achieve complete solitude, no matter how tempting the notion might be. Even with the entire staff gone he would still have Aunt Sarah and Vicar Humbly rattling through the house.

"Lady Faulconer will meet with the workers this afternoon," he grudgingly conceded.

"I fear, sir, that they are very insistent," Saunders persisted in apologetic tones. "They seem to have discovered a hidden door."

Gabriel bit back a descriptive curse. Lucifer's teeth. What did he care if they found a dozen hidden doors? All he wanted was a bit of privacy to make love to his wife.

"Do they presume this door is on the point of vanishing?" he demanded in exasperation.

"I cannot say, my lord."

Beneath him, Beatrice suddenly stirred, and he glanced down to discover a sudden glint in her eye.

"We should see what they have discovered," she said softly.

Gabriel briefly closed his eyes, his body shuddering in protest.

"Why did I know you would say that?" he groaned.

Her fingers skimmed over his bare chest. "Are you not intrigued?"

"I am very intrigued," he assured her, his smoldering gaze revealing that hidden doors and workmen were the last thing upon his mind. "Unfortunately, it seems I shall once again have to be patient."

"You are shameless," she chided, although she could not entirely hide her pleased smile.

"I do try," he murmured, then he turned his head back toward the closed door. "Tell them that we will be down in an hour, Saunders."

"Thank you, my lord."

With a rueful sigh Gabriel rolled onto his side. He would have an entire lifetime to share with this woman, he attempted to console his aching body. Endless nights to reveal the depths of his passion, and endless days to share the pleasure of her company. If she desired to see the blasted door, then that was precisely what they would do.

"Well, let us prepare to see this mysterious door," he said in resigned tones.

She sent him an encouraging smile. "Perhaps we shall find a hidden treasure."

Gabriel stilled before he abruptly leaned forward and claimed her lips in a swift, consuming kiss.

"I have already found my treasure," he whispered fiercely against her trembling lips.

Thirteen

Feeling as if she were in a dream, Beatrice allowed herself to be bathed and dressed in a pale buttercup gown. She heard none of her maid's chattering comments of the beauty of the day or the excitement of the workmen awaiting her arrival.

Instead, she meekly allowed herself to be dressed and her hair arranged as she basked in a glow of deep contentment.

Saints above. She had never expected to feel so . . . satisfied.

It was not just the pleasure that Gabriel had given to her. Although that had been wonderful, indeed. It was more the sheer intimacy between them. All of the barriers they had built between them had been suddenly shattered. They had been two vulnerable souls who had sought completion and found it beyond all expectation.

She had never felt so close to another, she acknowledged with an unwitting smile. There had been occasions during the night when it had been impossible to determine where she ended and Gabriel began. She had felt as if they were truly one. Two halves becoming a whole.

Did all women feel such a connection to their lovers? she wondered. Did they always experience such a thrilling sense of wonder and utter satisfaction?

She firmly suppressed an urge to laugh giddily.

It was hardly a subject she could discuss with others. Well, perhaps Addy or Victoria, she conceded. It would be interesting to discover their views of marriage and the marital bed.

A hint of revealing color touched her cheeks.

But not yet.

Her intimate emotions were too new, too vulnerable, to be discussed with anyone.

Anyone except Gabriel, she swiftly corrected. She now realized she could discuss anything with her husband. He was the one person who truly understood her. Who never made her feel foolish or awkward. Instead, he was patient and kind and so very tender.

Abruptly realizing she was staring into empty space as her maid regarded her with lifted brows, Beatrice gave herself a mental shake.

Good heavens, the servants would begin to fear she was daft if she continued to moon about in such a fashion.

Or worse, realize she was still in shock after a night spent in the arms of her husband.

That thought brought her abruptly to her feet. The last thing she desired was the servants gossiping about how she spent her nights.

Hoping that her cheeks were not as flushed as they felt, Beatrice swept calmly from the room and made her way down the hall to her husband's chambers. Not bothering to knock, she stepped inside to discover Gabriel standing before a mirror as he calmly tied his cravat.

Assuring herself Gabriel's valet had already been dismissed, she strolled to stand at his side. In the mirror their gazes met and Beatrice lifted a teasing brow.

"Good heavens, Gabriel, how long could it possibly take to tie a simple cravat?"

His lips twitched at her sudden ease in his company, but he made his expression stern.

"I shall have you know, my impatient wench, that a gentleman can devote several hours to achieving the perfect knot."

"Fustian." She wrinkled her nose at such foolishness. Thankfully Gabriel had never been one of those ridiculous dandies who wasted his days upon his attire. She had no patience with such coxcombs. "We are merely going downstairs, not having dinner with the Prince. What do the workmen care for your knot?"

"I am not trying to impress the workmen." He turned, reaching out to grasp her shoulders and pull her to face him. "I am attempting to impress my wife."

Familiar flutters raced through her as he gazed warmly down at her upturned countenance.

"Oh."

"Do you think she will approve?"

Beatrice slowly smiled, delighting in the manner he regarded her. Never had she considered herself beautiful. She had been a wallflower for too long not to fear she was displeasing to gentlemen. But last night Gabriel had taught her that she was indeed desirable.

"I believe she would approve no matter how your cravat was tied," she said huskily.

The hazel eyes glinted with pleasure. "Ah, but I especially wish to dazzle her."

"Indeed? And why is that?"

His hands gently traced the line of her shoulders. "Because she has made me an extraordinarily happy gentleman."

She shivered, breathing deeply of the warm scent that surrounded her. Already her knees were feeling decidedly weak.

"And how did she accomplish such a feat?"

"She has given me a gift beyond price."

"What gift?" she demanded in soft tones.

"Her trust."

Beatrice's heart halted before it staggered back to life with a jerky motion.

Why?

Why had she waited so long to put aside her anger?

Why had she punished both of them when it did nothing more than make her miserable?

Lifting her hand, she placed it against his cheek. "Yes."

His eyes darkened as he shifted to encircle her in his warm arms.

"And I wish her to know that I shall value her gift forever."

Feeling cherished and utterly safe in his embrace, she offered him a trembling smile.

"Will you?"

"Oh, yes." His arms tightened as a rather wicked expression touched his handsome features. "Do you know, my dear, I have a most delightful notion."

Beatrice chuckled, easily able to guess the direction of his thoughts.

In truth, her own thoughts were threatening to go down a similar path.

"What notion would that be?"

He brushed his lips over her brow. "That I forget my cravat and you forget the mysterious door and we both concentrate upon a more enticing means of spending our day."

Beatrice could not deny she was tempted. She did not doubt spending the day alone with Gabriel would be far more pleasurable than dealing with her workers. Unfortunately, the knowledge that all work upon the house would halt until she had inspected their discovery was bound to prey upon her mind.

Besides, she was curious about the door whether Gabriel was or not.

"But the workmen cannot continue until I give my approval," she said reluctantly.

He nuzzled the tender skin of her temple. "Then let them have a holiday."

She snuggled briefly against him before heaving a rueful sigh.

"You know, the sooner they finish their work, the sooner they will be gone from Falcon Park forever."

He pressed her tighter before stepping back with a grimace. Beatrice barely kept herself from tossing herself back into his arms and sending the workers to the devil.

Later, she silently promised herself.

They would have ample time to be together later.

She tingled in anticipation.

"Very well, you have made your point," he conceded with a faint smile. "Although I see that I shall have to have the grotto repaired with all possible speed. I must have some place of privacy with my wife. But only after I teach you to swim."

Oddly, the thought did not bring with it the usual panic. Perhaps her trial upon the storm-tossed water had helped to cure her terror. Not that she had any intention of testing her theory, she silently acknowledged. She was perfectly content to remain upon dry land like a sensible person.

"I fear it would be a hopeless task," she said firmly.

He sent her a telling look as he took her arm and led her from the room.

"I have discovered no task is hopeless," he informed her with a pointed glance.

She gave a sudden laugh. "True enough."

They moved toward the stairs at a leisurely pace, neither in a hurry to bring an end to their privacy.

"You know, I have been thinking." He at last broke the silence.

"A worthy task."

He flashed her a dry smile. "Yes. It occurs to me that we shall have to make a few arrangements to our chambers."

"But they were just refurbished," she retorted in startled tones.

"Quite nicely refurbished," he agreed, "but I do not desire to have you so far from me. I wish you in my bed at night and close at hand even when you are dressing."

Every night.

Her toes curled with delight.

"You are very demanding," she teased, not at all put out by his desire.

"I am indeed. And I have the perfect notion of what to do with your current chambers."

"What is that?"

"We shall have them made into a nursery."

Beatrice nearly tumbled down the stairs. "Oh."

Appearing not to notice her shock at the mere thought of carrying his child within her, Gabriel sent her an indulgent glance.

"I have come to know you very well, my little bully, and I do not believe for a moment you will allow your child to be hidden an entire floor away from you. Would it not be more sensible to have the nurse and baby just down the hall from us?"

Her shock slowly eased, and instead, a rather warm glow entered her heart.

She had not dared to allow herself to think of possessing children. Gabriel's children. It was far too painful. Now an odd longing stirred to life deep within her.

How extraordinary to have a baby growing within her.

To feel it move and breathe as it prepared to make its entrance into the world.

She might even now carry such a miracle within her.

A smile curved her lips. "Or we could have a bed prepared in your chambers. There is ample room."

"No, absolutely not," he declared firmly.

Well aware he would be as fiercely devoted to their child as herself, Beatrice did not fret at his refusal.

"We shall see."

"Minx," he chided, then, as he paused upon the landing, he gave a tilt of his head. "Ah, I believe I hear the babble of voices. This way."

Still holding her arm, they moved to enter the library, where several men stood in a circle, loudly voicing their views on what could be behind the hidden door. At their entrance, however, a sudden silence descended and the harried architect moved forward.

"My lady, thank goodness you have come."

"What is it?"

"We had just begun to remove the paneling, when we discovered the doorway. It is sealed and we did not wish to proceed without your approval."

"You did quite right. Thank you."

The man gave a pleased bow. "My pleasure, my lady."

With her curiosity fully piqued, Beatrice moved toward the door that was clearly visible without its cover of paneling. Set into the stone wall, it was small but obviously large enough to be entered. She ran her hands over the ancient wood, wondering who would have placed the door in the library and why.

She slanted a glance toward Gabriel, who had joined her.

"Did you know of this door?" she demanded.

He shook his head, although there was a rather bemused expression upon his countenance.

"Not precisely, but my mother often spoke of a secret cubby that she presumed to be a priest's hole."

"She never revealed it to you?" she questioned in surprise.

"No." He gave a low chuckle. "I believe she enjoyed watching me search for it when I was a child. It was one of the games we played when my father and brother were out hunting or losing our fortune at the card table." There was a short pause. "It is odd, though."

Beatrice lifted her brows. "What is?"

"When my mother laid upon her deathbed she called for me," he said, obviously dredging up memories long buried. "She told me to keep searching for the priest's hole."

A flare of excitement surged through her. Surely this had to be important for it to be upon Lady Faulconer's mind even upon her deathbed?

"Why did she not tell you where to find it?"

Gabriel shrugged. "I always assumed that she desired me to continue our pleasant game even though she would no longer be at my side. But perhaps . . ."

"What?" she prompted as his words trailed away.

"Perhaps she did not wish to reveal the secret before the servants."

"Yes," Beatrice breathed, her eyes shimmering. "Because she must have hidden something of value."

He gave a rueful shake of his head at her hopeful tone. "A charming notion, but highly doubtful. By that time my father had already run through his inheritance and was swiftly selling off my mother's jewels and any artwork worth a grout."

Not about to be discouraged, Beatrice offered him a challenging glance.

"There is only one means of discovering the truth."

"Yes." He turned to regard the door. "Shall we have the workmen break it open?"

"Oh, no, we do not want it destroyed," she protested in horror. "We shall search for the means to open it."

He regarded her flushed features before giving a sudden laugh. "You are enjoying this, are you not?"

"Well, it is rather exciting," she admitted. "Like something from one of those Gothic novels."

"If it were one of those Gothic novels, then you will no doubt discover a moldering skeleton behind the door and I shall be branded a murderer," he said in dry tones.

"Yes, indeed." She readily played along, ignoring the numerous workmen regarding their teasing banter with growing impatience. "Perhaps you are not Lord Faulconer at all. You might be an impostor who killed the true earl and hid his body in the priest's hole."

He merely grimaced at her accusation. "Unfortunately, I resemble my father too closely to deny he is my sire."

She pretended to be disappointed. "Yes, there is that."

"I am sorry. I fear that all we are bound to discover is a bounty of cobwebs and dust."

"Well, we will discover nothing simply standing here. Shall we begin our search?"

He offered her an elegant bow. "As you wish."

Moving in separate directions, they carefully began examining the walls, shelves, and even furniture for signs of a secret lever. It was exciting but at the same moment extraordinarily frustrating. She did not even know precisely what she was searching for and was well aware that she might overlook the key to opening the door a dozen times without even realizing what she had done.

A considerable number of moments passed before she impatiently moved aside a tall urn set beside the fireplace. The movement caught the edge of the tattered carpet, flipping it back to expose a small round stone set directly in the center of a flagstone.

"Here," she breathed softly.

In the blink of an eye, Gabriel was at her side. "What is it?"

She pointed to the stone. "It looks to be the lever."

"Since you are the one to discover it, it is only fitting that you perform the honors," he said with a smile.

Cautiously Beatrice reached out to press upon the stone, her heart racing as the stone easily slid downward. There was a faint groan behind her, and turning her head, she discovered the hidden door slowly opening.

"It worked," she cried in delight.

"Yes." Helping her to her feet, Gabriel glanced toward a nearby workman. "A candle, please."

"Yes, sir."

With hurried movements the young man fumbled with his flint, then, lighting a nearby candle, he handed it to Gabriel.

"Thank you." Holding Beatrice's arm, Gabriel moved to the door, stooping downward to make his way through the cramped opening. "Gads, I warned you there would be cobwebs."

Indifferent to the sticky strands that clung to her gown, Beatrice entered the chamber to glance around in interest. It was larger than she had expected, as large as her own dressing room, but disappointingly empty. Then the candle flickered and she caught sight of a heavy blanket covering something in the far corner.

She tugged at Gabriel's sleeve. "Look, there is something over there."

He smiled indulgently, although he regarded the thick dust upon the floor with a wrinkle of his nose.

"You will ruin your gown."

"It will not be the first," she retorted impatiently, moving toward the cover and dramatically tossing it aside. A cloud of dust briefly blinded her, then she gave a choked cry of disbelief. "Oh."

"What is it?" Gabriel moved hurriedly forward, only to halt as the candlelight fell upon the piles of pictures, statues, silver, and jewelry boxes. "Good God."

With shaking hands Beatrice lowered herself and reached out to grasp one of the framed pictures with reverent care.

"I told you we would find a treasure."

"You did indeed," Gabriel agreed in distracted tones, reaching to pick up one of the carved boxes and flipping open the lid to reveal a magnificent diamond necklace complete with tiara and heavy bracelets. "My mother's jewels."

Still sifting through the numerous canvases, Beatrice asked in wonderment. "How did they get here? Your father?"

He gave a sharp laugh. "Gads, no. If my father had known of these, he would have sold them long ago."

"Then your mother?"

"It must have been."

"But why?"

Gabriel cast a bemused glance over the priceless mound of bounty.

"I suppose she realized that my father and brother were determined to bring the estate to ruin and she did what she could to preserve a few of the more notable heirlooms."

Notable, indeed, Beatrice acknowledged, easily able to detect the work of a master hand.

"These are Rubenses and that is a Van Dyke. Dear heavens, they are worth a fortune."

"Yes." He gave a slow, disbelieving shake of his head. "All this time I have blamed my father for depriving Falcon Park of its treasures, and they have been here all along."

Beatrice sat back on her heels, absently brushing a cobweb from her cheek.

"Surely your father must have been suspicious when these items disappeared?"

Even in the muted candlelight Beatrice could detect the sudden hardening of Gabriel's features.

"No doubt he presumed it was the work of my brother, or even that he had sold them himself in a drunken stupor. He once called in the magistrate to find his stolen carriage and precious bays, only to learn he had lost them in a game of hazard the evening before."

She reached out to lightly touch his hand. "Your mother was very wise."

He clutched her hand, an odd glitter suddenly shimmering in the hazel eyes.

"She has given me the inheritance that I thought lost forever. It is truly amazing."

Beatrice stilled at his fierce words, suddenly struck by the rather terrible irony of the situation.

"Yes."

Perhaps sensing her air of reserve, he regarded her with a faint frown.

"What is it, Beatrice?"

"I was just thinking . . ."

"What?"

She was forced to clear an odd lump that threatened to settle in her throat.

"Had your mother revealed her secret, you would never have been forced to wed me."

He stiffened as the truth in her words sank in.

"No, I would not have. I had the means of saving Falcon Park in my own hands."

Perhaps expecting him to dismiss her words with a

teasing grin, Beatrice discovered her heart flinching in pain.

"Yes," she said in low tones, desperately wishing she could read his thoughts.

For a moment he merely regarded his unexpected treasure in silence, then without warning he straightened and wiped his hands upon a handkerchief.

"You must excuse me, my dear."

Struck by a ridiculous sense of panic, Beatrice scrambled to her feet.

"Where are you going?"

"I have something I must do."

"Now?"

"It cannot wait another moment," he retorted in firm tones, leaning forward to brush a hasty kiss upon her cheek. "I shall see you later."

Clutching her skirts with stiff fingers, Beatrice watched his hurried departure with a sudden chill.

Something had changed within Gabriel.

Something that she feared might very well alter their relationship forever.

Fourteen

The day seemed interminable.

Despite her determination not to dwell upon Gabriel's abrupt departure, Beatrice discovered it an impossible task.

Seated in her study, she found her thoughts returning time and time again to earlier that morning.

There had been no doubt that Gabriel had been shocked by the unexpected find.

Perhaps even a bit shaken at the realization that such a vast fortune had been nearly lost forever.

But what deep thoughts had caused that peculiar gleam in his eye?

And what had sent him fleeing from her with such haste?

It was ridiculous to brood upon the unanswerable questions, but with traitorous insistence the fears began to bloom within her heart.

What if Gabriel were devastated when he realized he had tied himself irrevocably to a woman he no longer needed?

What if he suddenly realized that she was a burden he could do without?

What if he had decided that a lawyer could put a swift end to a marriage he had been forced into?

Rather desperately she attempted to assure herself she was being absurd.

Of course Gabriel was surprised, and maybe even bemused, by his sudden windfall. And perhaps he had needed time to accept that he was not the penniless earl he had once thought.

That certainly did not mean his feelings toward her had altered in any way.

With grim determination she had forced herself to recall their glorious evening together.

He had not pretended the impassioned kisses or trembling caresses. Nor had he pretended the tender embrace that had kept her warm and content through the night.

Surely he had to feel something for her? she assured herself rather desperately.

She could not lose her faith in him now.

Eager to keep the fluttering sense of panic at bay, Beatrice at last went in search of the housekeeper. Perhaps the older woman had some notion of her husband's whereabouts.

After a lengthy traipse through the vast house, Beatrice at last discovered Mrs. Greene in the back parlor, where she was instructing a maid on the proper means of scrubbing the fireplace.

At her entrance, the housekeeper turned to cross to her side.

"Good afternoon, my lady."

"Ah, Mrs. Greene, have you seen Lord Faulconer?" she asked in what she hoped was a casual tone.

Not surprisingly, the woman said, "No, my lady."

"What of Vicar Humbly?"

"I fear I have not seen him since breakfast."

Beatrice frowned in uneasy bewilderment.

Where the devil could they be?

"It is very odd that they have gone without leaving a message as to where they might be."

The older woman appeared remarkably unconcerned, even going so far as to lift one shoulder.

"No doubt they are visiting a tenant, or merely inspecting the fields."

Perfectly reasonable explanations, but Beatrice was not comforted. She simply could not dismiss that expression upon Gabriel's countenance when he had left her.

Had it been anger?

Disgust?

Pleasure?

It was annoyingly impossible to know for certain.

"Perhaps they informed Aunt Sarah of their destination," she at last muttered.

"I believe Mrs. Quarry has gone to the village," the older woman offered.

"On her own?" Beatrice demanded in shock. Aunt Sarah never left the estate without Gabriel or herself in tow.

"Yes, my lady."

"How extraordinary."

Clearing her throat, the housekeeper cast a deliberate glance toward the Louis XIV clock upon the mantel.

"If you will excuse me, my lady, I should see to the linen."

Realizing that she was keeping the busy servant from her duties, Beatrice gave a reluctant nod of her head.

"Of course."

With dragging steps she turned back into the hallway and made her way to the library to check the progress of her secretary. Although it had only been two hours since she had requested Mr. Eaton to begin cataloguing the contents of the priest's hole, she had to find some means of occupying her thoughts or she might very well go mad.

With a nod toward the two footmen who had been wisely set beside the hidden door for security, Beatrice stepped inside the small chamber.

With his usual efficiency, Mr. Eaton had set up several candelabra to provide an adequate amount of light as well as a chair and writing table to aid in his work.

At her entrance, however, he set aside the table and jumped to his feet.

"Welcome, my lady."

"How do you come along?" she demanded, noting he had already separated the bounty into several neat piles. Her methodical mind silently approved of his orderly technique.

"Very well," he retorted, his pale face uncommonly flushed with obvious excitement. "There is quite the finest collection of Rubenses it has ever been my privilege to view, and I am fairly certain that the silver can be traced to Charles the First. I have not yet examined the jewels, but I do not doubt they will prove to be priceless."

She briefly regarded the numerous boxes that spilled over with diamonds, rubies, and emeralds.

"Priceless, indeed. And to think they have been hiding here for years."

"It is most astonishing. Lord Faulconer is a fortunate gentleman. There are few in all of England who can boast of such a fine collection."

"Fortunate? I wonder if he believes so," she muttered.

Mr. Eaton gave a startled blink. "Pardon me?"

"Nothing," said dismissively. "Continue with your work."

"Certainly."

Still plagued by her sense of restlessness, Beatrice left the priest's hole and crossed out of the library.

Now what?

She supposed she could always visit Mrs. Litton. Or perhaps she should simply return to her chambers and enjoy a brief rest. She had, after all, been kept awake most of the night.

A tingle of warmth rushed through her at the sudden memory of precisely how she had been kept awake.

No.

She was in no mood for a quiet rest. She needed something that would firmly take her mind off Gabriel.

As if in answer to her unspoken plea, a uniformed footman suddenly appeared to offer her a bow.

"Pardon me, my lady."

"Yes?"

"I have a message from Vicar Humbly."

She gave a started blink at the unexpected words. "A message?"

"Yes. He requests that you meet him at the church."

Beatrice could not imagine what the vicar would be doing at the church. Nor why he would send a message for her to meet him there.

It simply made no sense.

"Did he say what he desired?"

"No, my lady, only that you join him as swiftly as possible."

"Very well."

Leaving the footman, Beatrice retrieved her spenser and bonnet before she escaped from the house. Even though she could not make head or tail of Mr. Humbly's odd behavior, she might as well be walking to the church as to be pacing the floor in her chambers.

Beatrice breathed in deeply as she crossed the courtyard and made her way toward the path that would lead to the nearby church and vicarage.

The day was fine with only a hint of dampness in the breeze. It felt good to have the pale sunshine warming her body and to smell the unmistakable scent of wildflowers just coming into bloom. Her stiff tension began to ease as she forced herself to appreciate the beauty about her. With Gabriel confined to his bed, it had been far too long since she had enjoyed a simple stroll.

Slowing her steps to a mere snail's pace, it took some time to reach the grounds surrounding the church. At last, however, she stepped through the fringe of trees that surrounded the yard, only to come to a startled halt as Gabriel suddenly appeared before her.

"Gabriel." She regarded him in a wary manner, uncertain what to expect. It did not help that his dark features were once again impossible to read. "What are you doing here?"

"Awaiting you, my dear."

"Me? I thought Vicar Humbly had sent me the message."

"He sent the note for me."

Beatrice desperately searched his guarded expression for some hint of his inner thoughts. She felt as vulnerable as if she were once again on that storm-tossed lake, at the mercy of unseen forces.

"Why?" she breathed unsteadily.

"Because I have prepared a surprise for you."

"A surprise?"

"Yes." He smiled deep into her troubled eyes. "And on this occasion I intend to do things right."

Before Beatrice could question his mysterious words, he suddenly dropped to one knee and grasped her hands in his own.

"Gabriel . . . whatever are you doing?"

He offered her that wicked grin she had come to love so dearly.

"I intend to propose to you."

"Propose?" She gave a disbelieving shake of her head. "But we are already wed."

He gave her fingers a swift squeeze. "Beatrice, a gentleman cannot possibly propose in style if you insist on being so prosaically practical," he complained.

"I do not understand," she said even as her renegade heart began to swell with hope.

His expression slowly sobered. "My dear, during my first proposal we both know that I was not entirely truthful with you."

She looked away, not wishing to speak of the past.

"Gabriel, there is no need for this."

"There is for me," he insisted. "On this occasion I come to you as a gentleman well able to provide you with all the luxuries you may desire. I have an estate that is in need of restoration, but with a fine collection of art and the promise of a bountiful harvest. I can also offer you a king's ransom in diamonds, rubies, emeralds, and sapphires to grace your beauty. And this . . . " With an elegant motion he reached into his pocket to remove a ring. Beatrice watched in wonderment as he slowly slid the large square-cut diamond onto her finger and raised her hand to his lips to brush a lingering kiss upon her palm.

She shivered, rather afraid that she must be dreaming.

Surely nothing so wonderful could happen to Beatrice Chaswell?

Of course, if she were dreaming, she desperately hoped that no one bothered to awaken her.

"It is beautiful," she breathed.

"It belonged to my grandmother."

"I do not know what to say."

He slowly rose to his feet, appearing like a prince of old with the sunlight shimmering within his russet hair and adding a hint of bronze to his lean features.

"I ask you to be my wife, Beatrice, not for Falcon Park or hungry tenants, but for me. Just me."

"Oh, Gabriel."

He lifted her hands to press them to his heart. "I also have a confession."

She asked bemusedly, "What confession?"

"The fact that I was in need of your inheritance was not all that I hid from you."

"What do you mean?"

"I mean that I wanted you to be my wife because I loved you."

Beatrice's heart faltered in disbelief at his low words. "What?"

"Oh, I did not realize the emotion for what it was," he admitted. "I knew only that when I was in your company I felt comfortable and oddly content. No other maiden had ever done more than make me wish to flee miles away."

"We are very much alike," she said in husky tones.

"No, it was more than that. Somehow I knew that we were meant to be together. There was a bond I could not explain."

Her eyes abruptly filled with tears of joy.

Yes.

There had been a bond from the moment their eyes had met.

A connection that transcended logic. As if fate itself had determined they were destined for each other.

"I felt so too."

That wicked smile returned. "And, of course, there has always been the desperate manner I have desired you."

Beatrice thought she might burst from sheer happiness.

"You truly love me?"

"I have loved you since the day we met," he assured her. "But at first I denied what my heart whispered, and then, when you discovered the truth of our marriage, I told myself that I was unworthy of such an emotion."

Beatrice gently reached up to lay her hand upon his cheek. "I tried to convince myself that as well. But no matter how I tried to remain furious with you, my heart was breaking."

"No more," Gabriel said in firm tones. "The past is behind us. Today we will say our vows again and start our marriage as it was meant to be."

Her eyes widened with startled pleasure. "You wish to wed again?"

"Vicar Humbly is awaiting us in the church to perform the ceremony."

Beatrice tilted back her head to give a joyous laugh. "I wondered where he had disappeared to."

"He has been helping me to prepare my surprise. So tell me, Beatrice, will you marry me?"

She did not hesitate as she threw herself against his warm body.

"Yes. Oh, yes."

Twirling her about, Gabriel at last set her on her feet and together they ran laughing toward the church.

Beatrice was quite certain that she could not possibly be any happier than she was at that moment.

She had the man she loved at her side and they had their whole future to look forward to.

Then she stepped into the church and she tumbled into love with Gabriel all over again.

Her disbelieving gaze traveled over the mounds of daisies that had been banked along the aisle, while the pews were filled with smiling tenants who let out a loud cheer at the entrance of their beloved earl. At the altar a clearly delighted Vicar Humbly gave her a warm glance as Aunt Sarah and the servants crowded behind him with baskets of grain to toss at the bride and groom.

Tears of pleasure once again filled her eyes. "Oh, my."

"You are pleased?" Gabriel whispered close to her ear.

"It is perfect," she assured him with a brilliant smile.

"As it should be." He lowered his head to press a tender kiss to her lips. "Come, the vicar awaits us."

With surprising stealth for a gentleman of his girth, Vicar Humbly slipped down the stairs and made his way to the foyer.

He was not precisely sneaking away, he assured himself. After all, he had made his good-byes to both Gabriel and Beatrice the night before. There was no need to trouble the two when they so clearly desired to be alone. It would be far better to quietly slip away in the carriage Gabriel had insisted take him back to Surrey.

Wrestling with his large bag that threatened to knock over the various urns and pier tables that lined the foyer, Humbly had nearly reached the door, when the voice he had been dreading cut shrilly through the air.

"Oh, Vicar Humbly."

Rolling his eyes heavenward, Humbly reluctantly turned to face the determined widow.

Blast.

He had been so very close to freedom.

"Yes, Mrs. Quarry?"

Hurrying forward, she clamped her hands upon his arms as if realizing he would bolt if possible.

"Surely you do not mean to travel in such dismal weather?" she demanded.

Now that his task was accomplished, Humbly would gladly have traveled through a blizzard to return to the peace of his vicarage. As much as he might love Gabriel and Beatrice, he was eager to be far from the wiles of this desperate woman.

"A spot of rain, nothing more," he assured her with a shrug.

"But I have ordered your favorite duck in cherry sauce to be prepared for dinner," she attempted to sway him. "Cook will be most disappointed."

"I fear that I really must be on my way."

She gave a sudden pout. "Nonsense. What could be so urgent?"

"I . . . well . . . I must prepare to move into my cottage before the arrival of the new vicar," he hurriedly stammered.

With bewildering speed, her tight expression melted and she was batting her lashes in a most peculiar fashion.

"Oh, yes, your dear cottage," she cooed. "How envious you have made me. I should very much like to visit this cottage of yours."

Humbly gave a choked cough. "It is quite ordinary, I assure you."

Her fingers dug painfully into his arm. "Perhaps Gabriel and Beatrice will wish to visit you."

"Perhaps," he agreed, well aware that it would be several months before Gabriel and Beatrice would desire to leave the privacy of Falcon Park. "Now, I really must be leaving."

Dramatically moving her hands to her narrow bosom, the older woman gave a sharp cry.

"Oh, how I hate partings. Good-bye, my dear, dear Vicar. Do not forget me."

"Ah, yes, excuse me."

Hurrying through the door before the woman could

create a further scene, Humbly breathed a thankful sigh at the sight of the waiting carriage.

Salvation, at last.

"A very tender parting, Humbly. I fear you have broken poor Aunt Sarah's heart."

Abruptly turning his head, Humbly discovered Lord and Lady Faulconer standing upon the bottom step. A pleased smile touched his countenance at the sight of them arm in arm.

"Do not tease Mr. Humbly, dear," Beatrice chided with a tender glance at her husband.

Humbly gave a click of his tongue. "Goodness, you should not be standing in the rain," he protested even as a warmth filled his heart. He had never seen Beatrice appear happier, and there was a new air of deep contentment that had settled about Gabriel. The brittle pain had been laid to rest.

Beatrice gave a lift of her brows. "You did not believe we would allow you to leave without saying good-bye?"

"Indeed, not," Gabriel swiftly added. "We have so much to thank you for."

Humbly waved aside their gratitude with an embarrassed flush. "No, no. I have done nothing."

Gabriel placed an arm about his wife's shoulders with a wry smile.

"You have performed no less than a miracle. You have convinced two stubborn, thick-skulled fools to admit their love."

"I am delighted you are so happy." He regarded Beatrice with a searching gaze. "It is all I have ever wished for you."

"I am happy," she assured him, a delighted color filling her cheeks. "Far happier than I ever dreamed possible. Thanks to you."

He reached out to pat her hand. "Just remember to always listen to your heart, my dear. It will never lead you astray."

"I will," she promised.

"And if she forgets, I shall haul her off to the grotto and swiftly remind her," Gabriel teased with a wicked smile.

She gave a choked laugh, but Humbly did not miss the shimmering heat that filled the amber eyes.

"Gabriel."

"A fine notion," Humbly agreed, knowing his time to leave had arrived. He performed his most elegant bow. "Now I must be off to Surrey."

Allowing the waiting groom to take his bag, Humbly moved toward the carriage. The steps were being lowered, when the voice of Mrs. Quarry could be heard from the shadowed foyer.

"Vicar. Oh, Vicar."

"Good heavens." Humbly shoved his bulk into the carriage, indifferent to the amused expression of the groom.

"Vicar, I have packed you some nice cucumber sandwiches."

Leaning out the window, Humbly waved an impatient hand at the startled driver.

"To Surrey, my son," he called in urgent tones. "And be quick about it."

With a crack of the whip they were off, and Humbly heaved a deep sigh of relief.

Surely Cupid had never been plagued with tenacious widows and cucumber sandwiches?

It was almost enough to put him off matchmaking once and for all.

A sudden smile curved his lips.

Well, perhaps not yet, he silently conceded.

After all, there was still Victoria and . . .

ABOUT THE AUTHOR

Debbie Raleigh lives with her family in Missouri. She is currently working on her next Zebra Regency romance, *A Scandalous Marriage,* which will be published in March 2003. Debbie loves to hear from readers, and you may write to her c/o Zebra Books. Please include a self-addressed stamped envelope if you wish a response.

More Zebra Regency Romances

BOOK YOUR PLACE ON OUR WEBSITE AND MAKE THE READING CONNECTION!

We've created a customized website just for our very special readers, where you can get the inside scoop on everything that's going on with Zebra, Pinnacle and Kensington books.

When you come online, you'll have the exciting opportunity to:

- View covers of upcoming books
- Read sample chapters
- Learn about our future publishing schedule (listed by publication month *and author*)
- Find out when your favorite authors will be visiting a city near you
- Search for and order backlist books from our online catalog
- Check out author bios and background information
- Send e-mail to your favorite authors
- Meet the Kensington staff online
- Join us in weekly chats with authors, readers and other guests
- Get writing guidelines
- AND MUCH MORE!

**Visit our website at
http://www.kensingtonbooks.com**